KORGi

CREATED BY

ANN & CHRISTIAN SLADE

top Shelf ™
PRODUCTIONS

CHRISTIAN SLADE

KORGi

BOOK 2

TOP SHELF PRODUCTIONS

KORGI (BOOK 2): THE COSMIC COLLECTOR © & ™ 2008 CHRISTIAN SLADE.

Published by
Top Shelf Productions
PO Box 1282
Marietta, GA 30061-1282
USA

Editor-in-Chief: Chris Staros

Top Shelf Productions is an imprint of IDW Publishing, a division of Idea and Design Works, LLC. Offices: 2765 Truxtun Road, San Diego, CA 92106. Top Shelf Productions®, the Top Shelf logo, Idea and Design Works®, and the IDW logo are registered trademarks of Idea and Design Works, LLC. All Rights Reserved. This is a work of fiction. Any similarities to persons living or dead are purely coincidental. With the exception of small excerpts of artwork used for review purposes, none of the contents of this publication may be reprinted without the permission of IDW Publishing. IDW Publishing does not read or accept unsolicited submissions of ideas, stories, or artwork.

Visit our online catalog at
www.topshelfcomix.com.

ISBN 978-1-60309-010-0

Printed in Korea

20   19   18   17   6   5   4   3

Thanks to Chris, Brett
and the Top Shelf family

Fellow artist friends
Brad, J Pat, Ken, Mike, and Ray

Janice, Deb, Kandee, Art & Pat, Thyra
and all the corgi people who have
supported my work over the years

Special thanks to my family.
Especially, Mom, Dad, Maggie, David,
Ann, Kate & Nate

Extra special thanks to
Queenie, Will, Wanda, Penny, Leo
and all the Welsh Corgis in the world

Thank you
for helping me find Korgi!

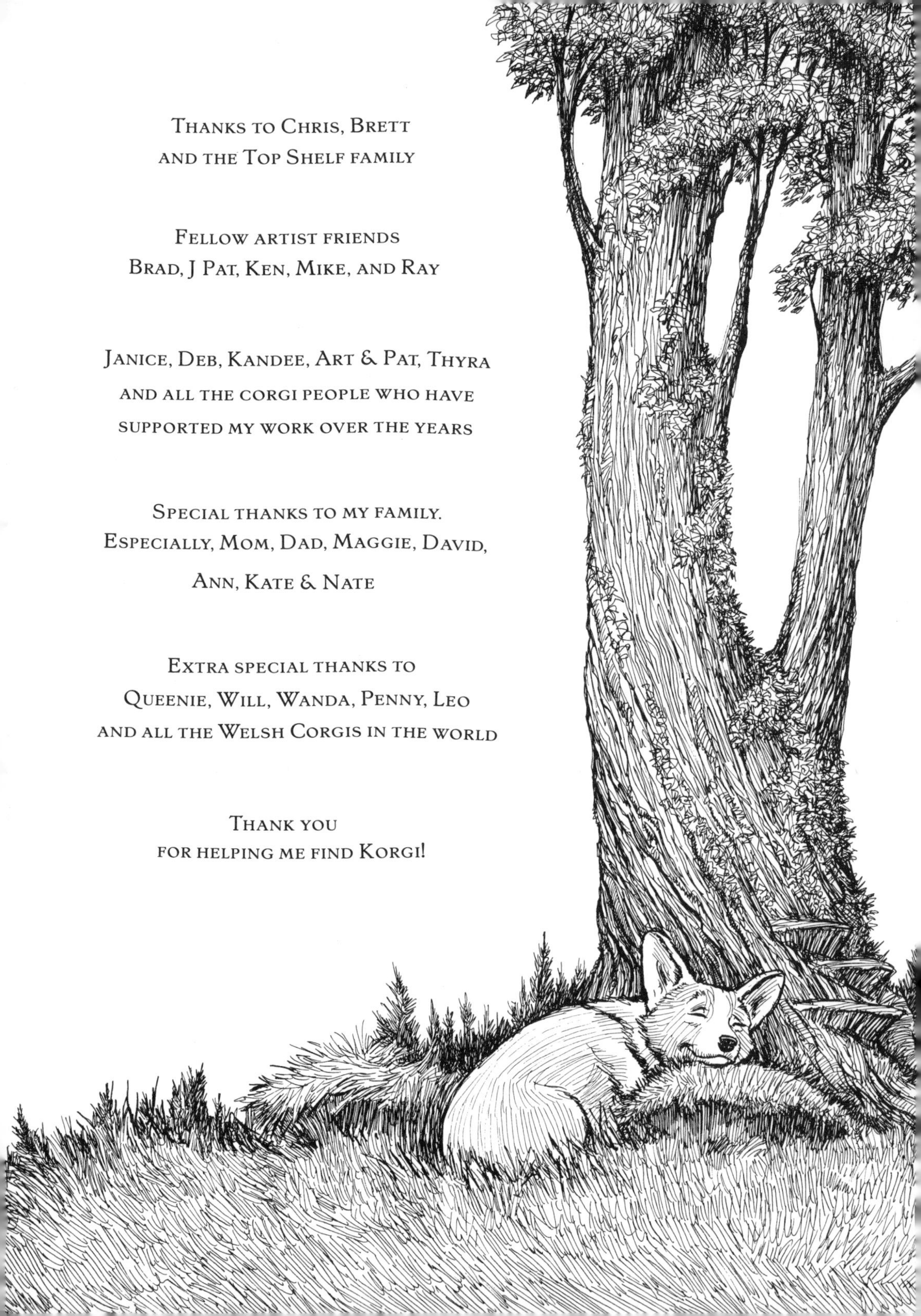

2

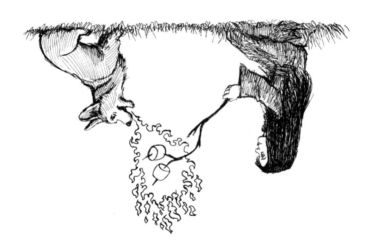

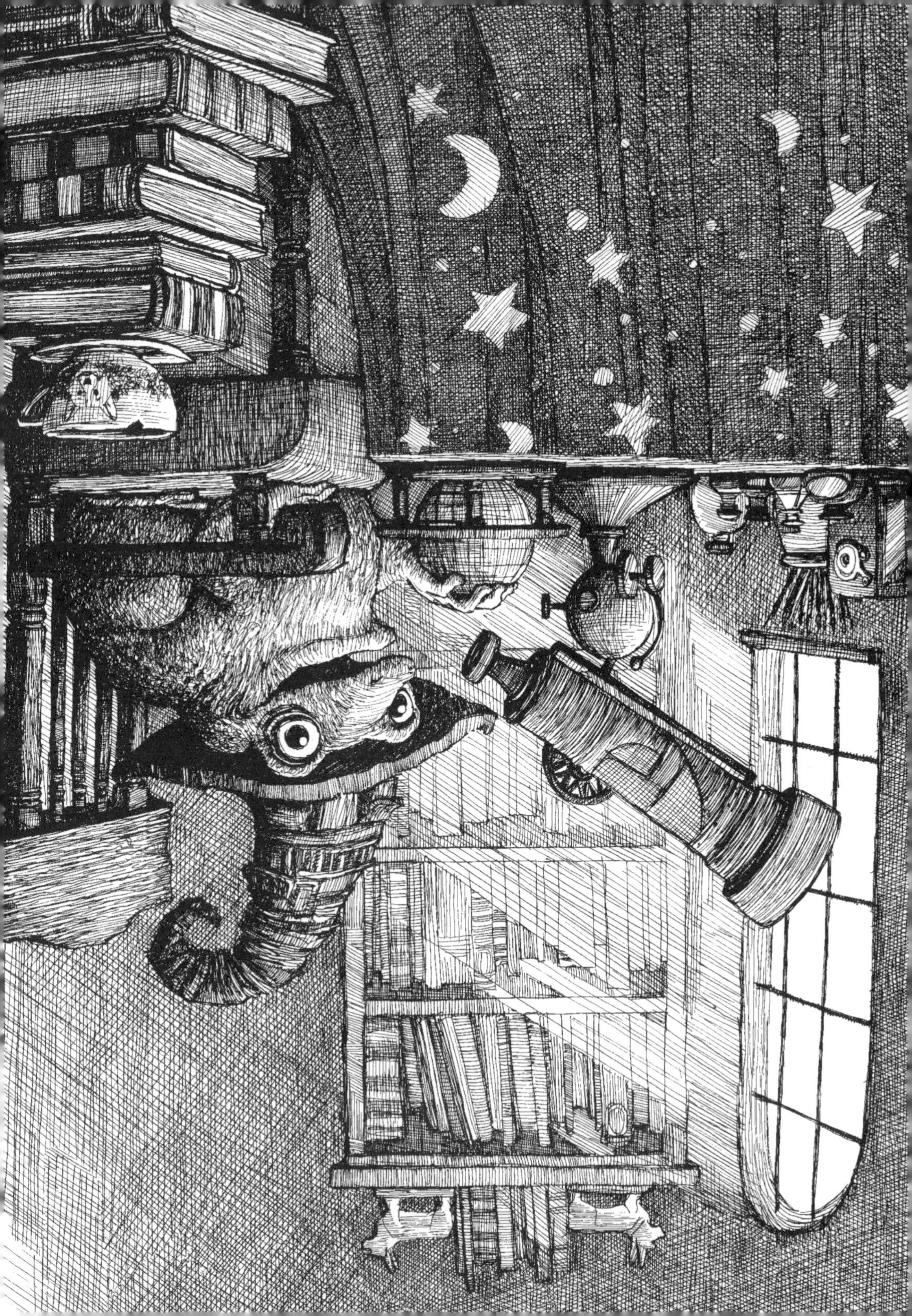

WELCOME BACK, Dear Reader! I knew I'd be seeing you again soon. Much has come to pass in our woodland town since last we met. Mollies have continued to do remarkable things alongside their magical Korgi friends . . . But strange happenings are afoot. Some of us with the gift of flight have lost our wings. They've not been shed by accident, mind you.

No, these wings have been stolen by a variety of clever traps.

The Hollow is filled with scared whispers concerning this new enemy who has yet to be seen.

Today, young Ivy — who still has her wings — and her gifted Korgi cub, Sprout, will bravely journey the surrounding land in search of clues to this mystery.

So grab a hot cup of drink, sit back, and enjoy the tale of,

"THE COSMIC COLLECTOR"

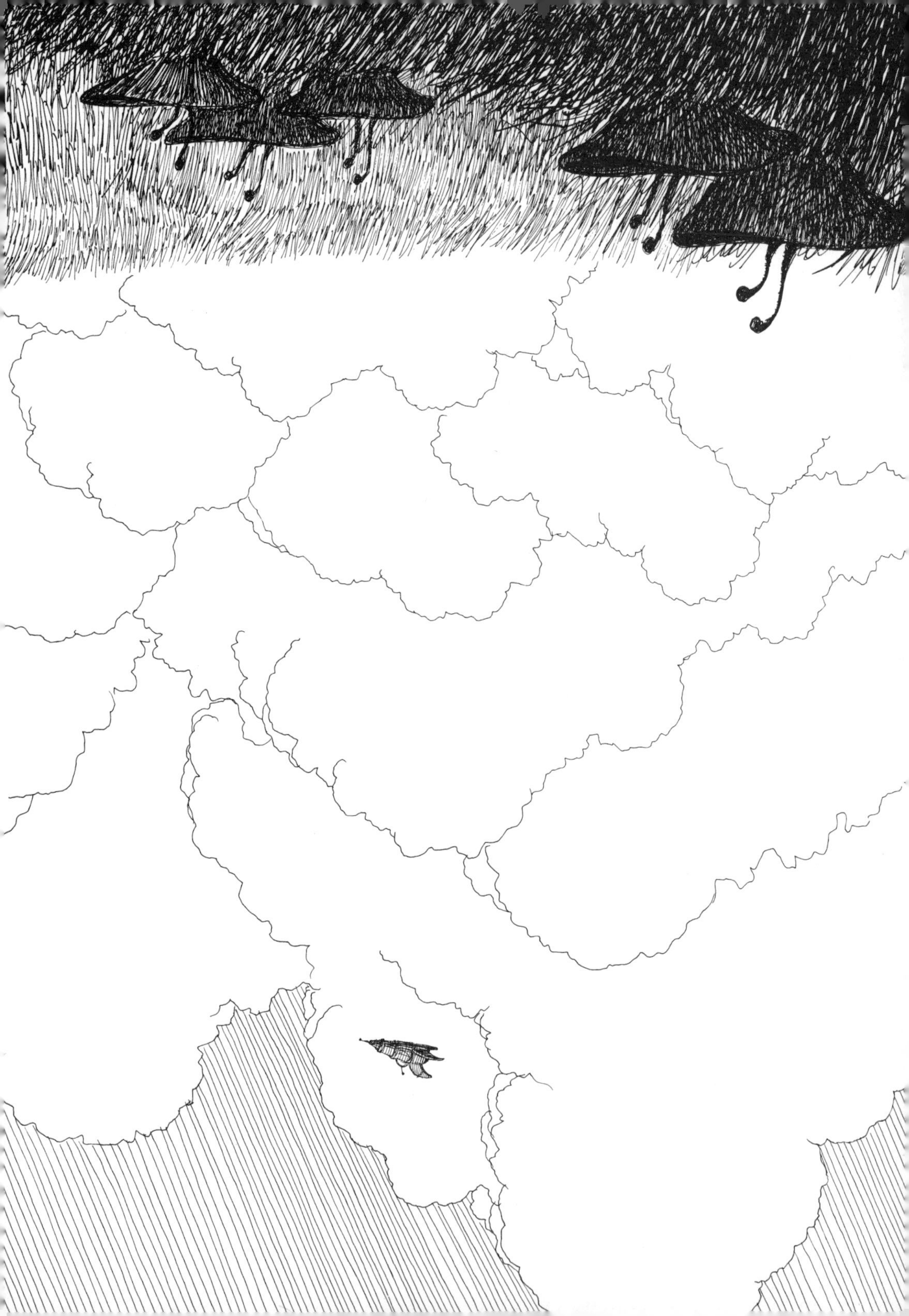

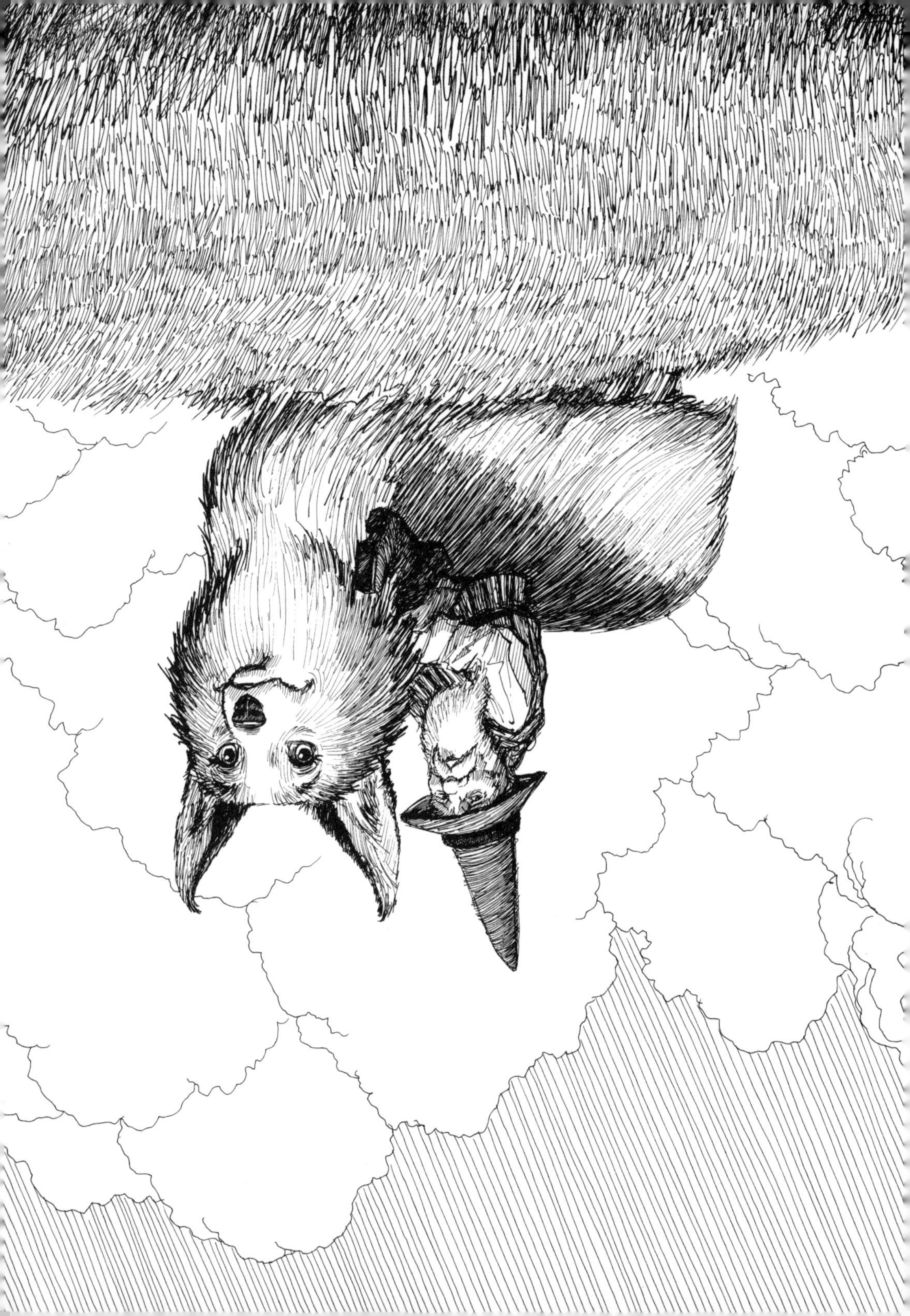

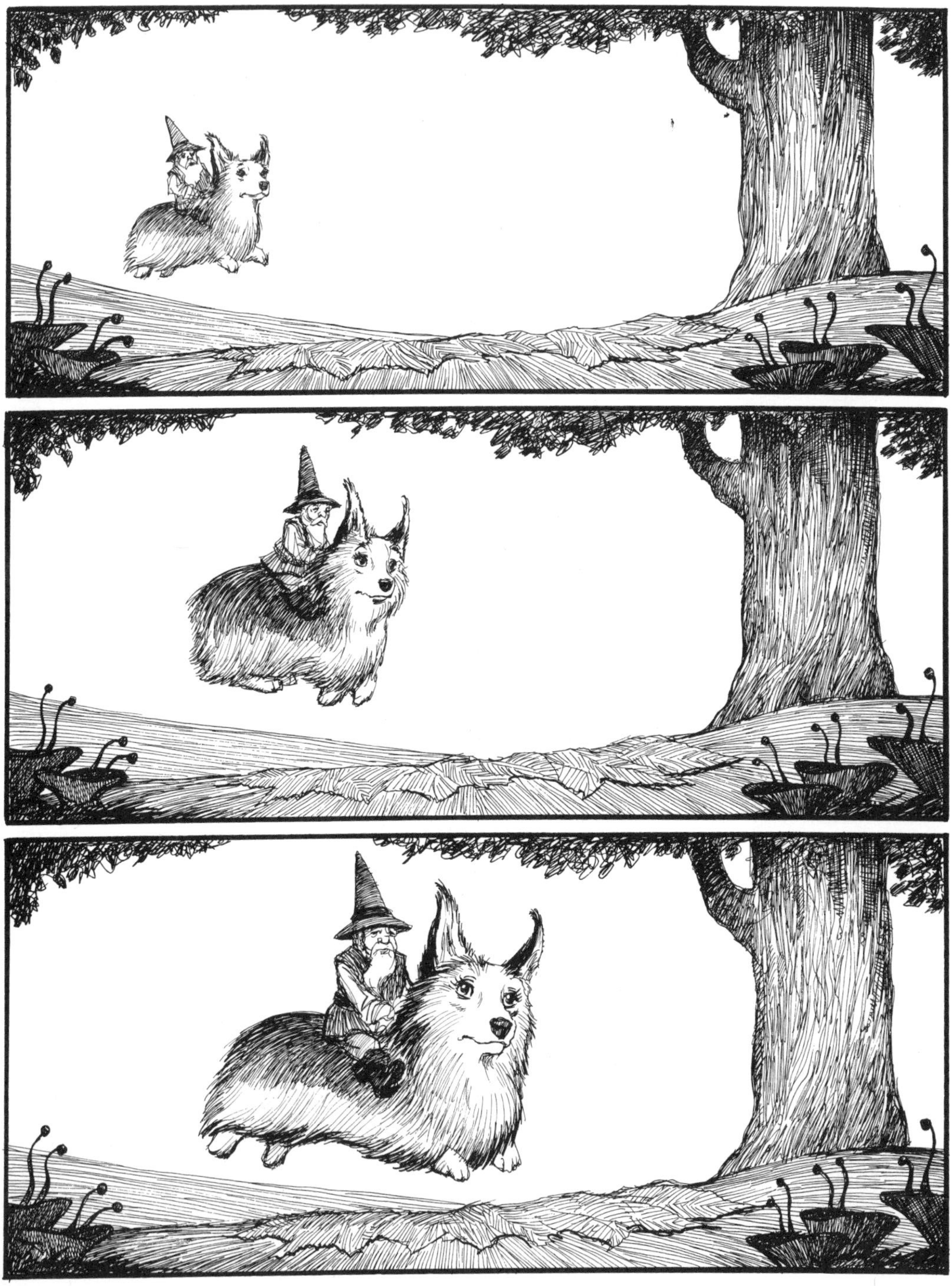

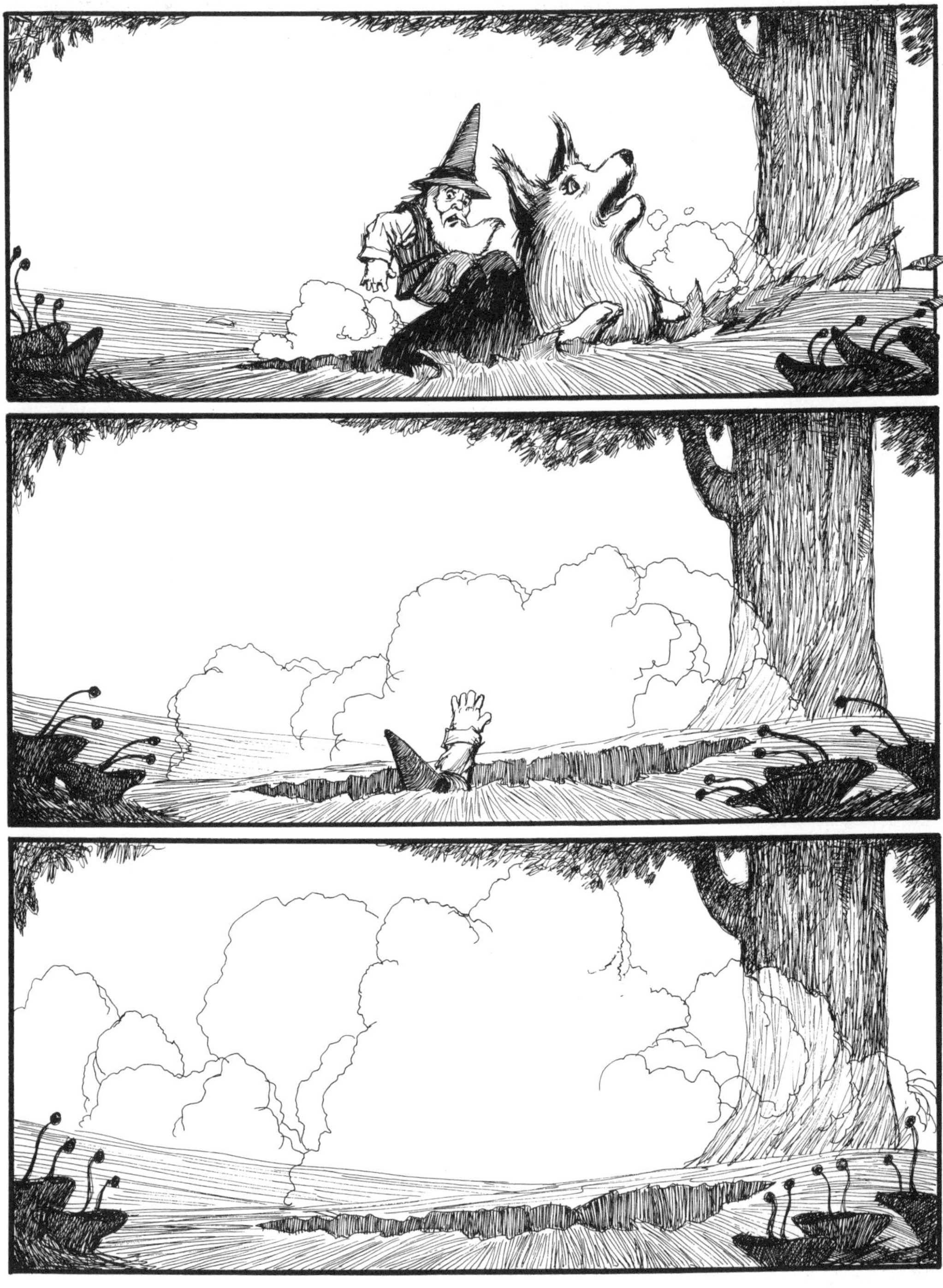

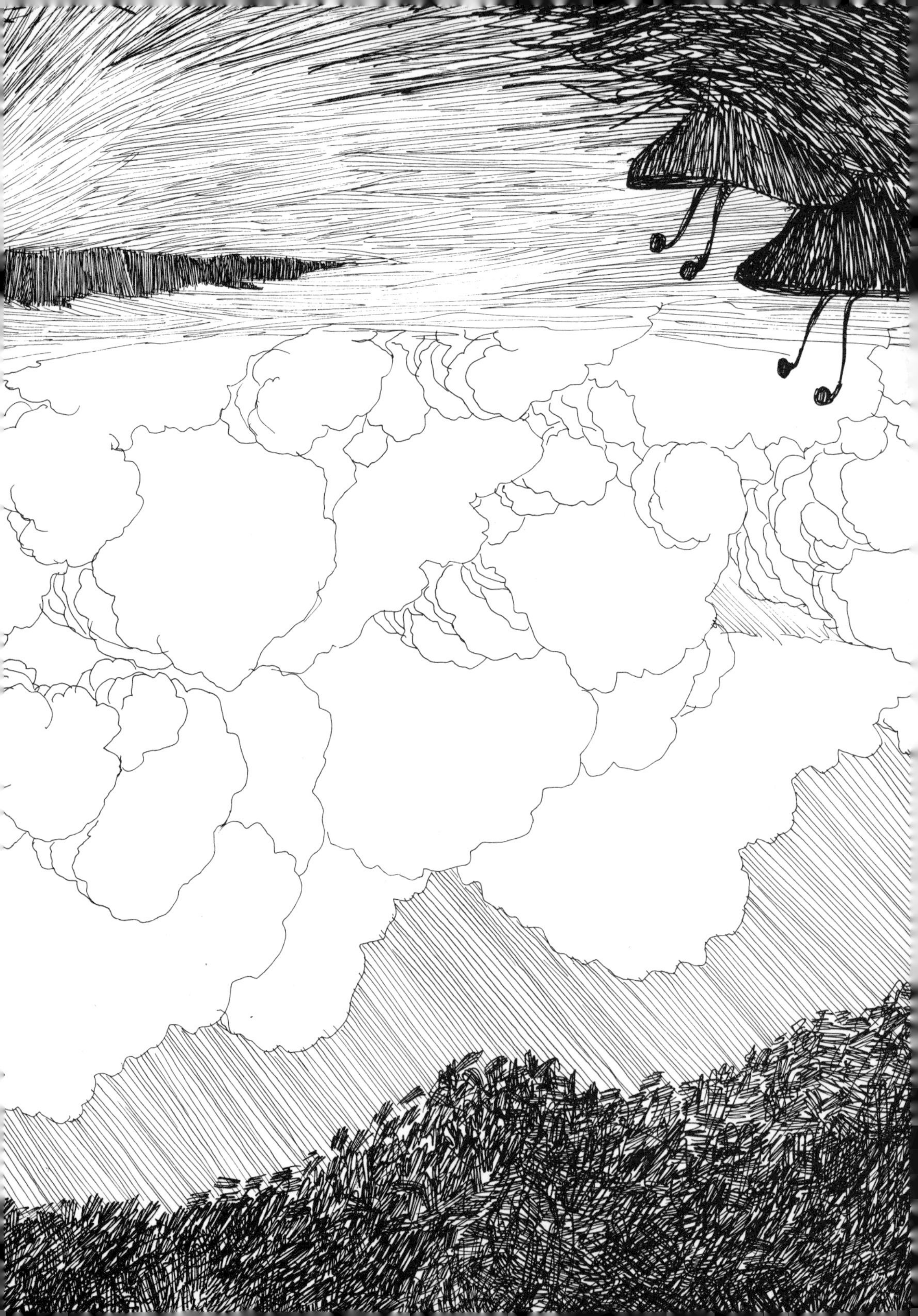

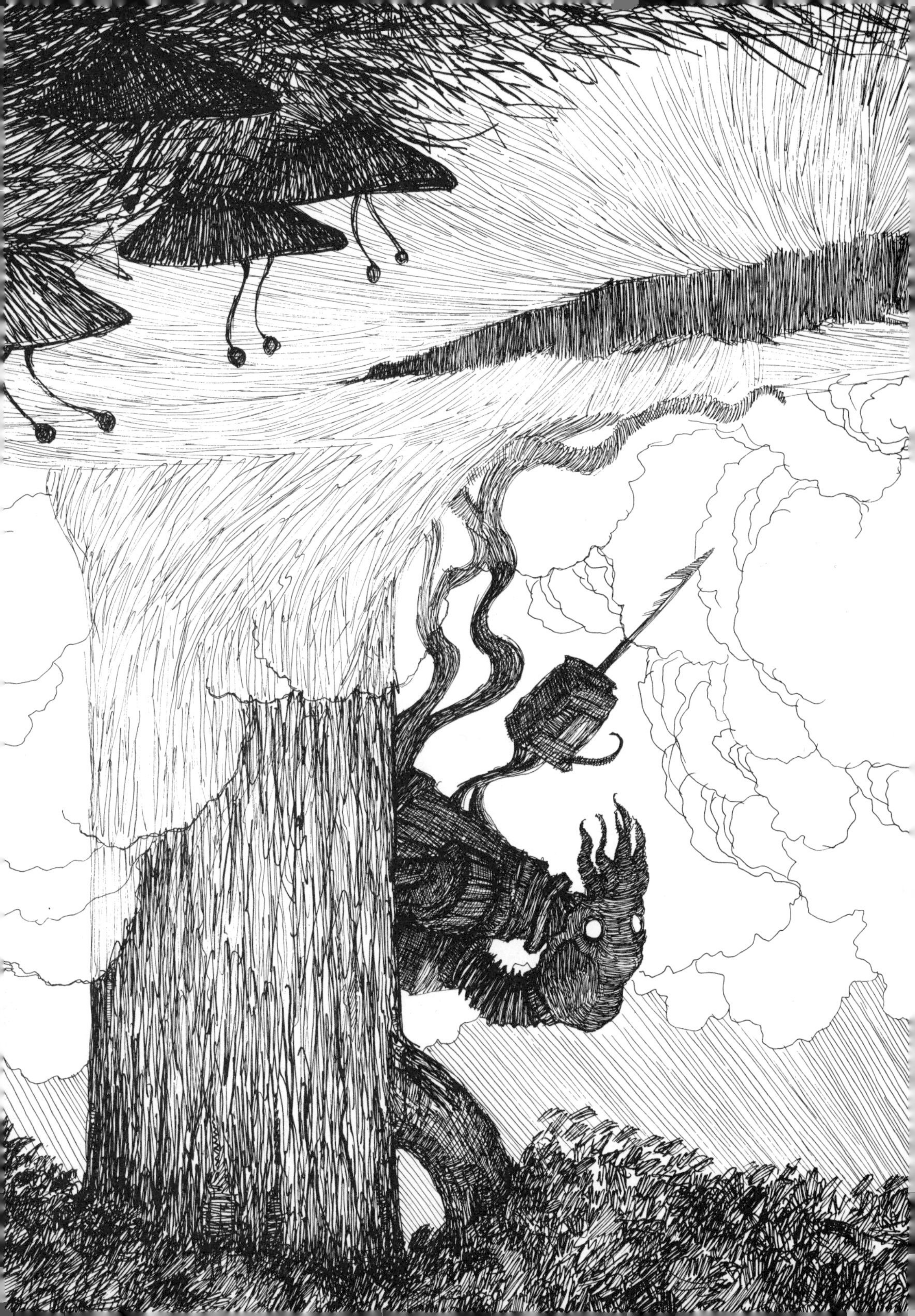

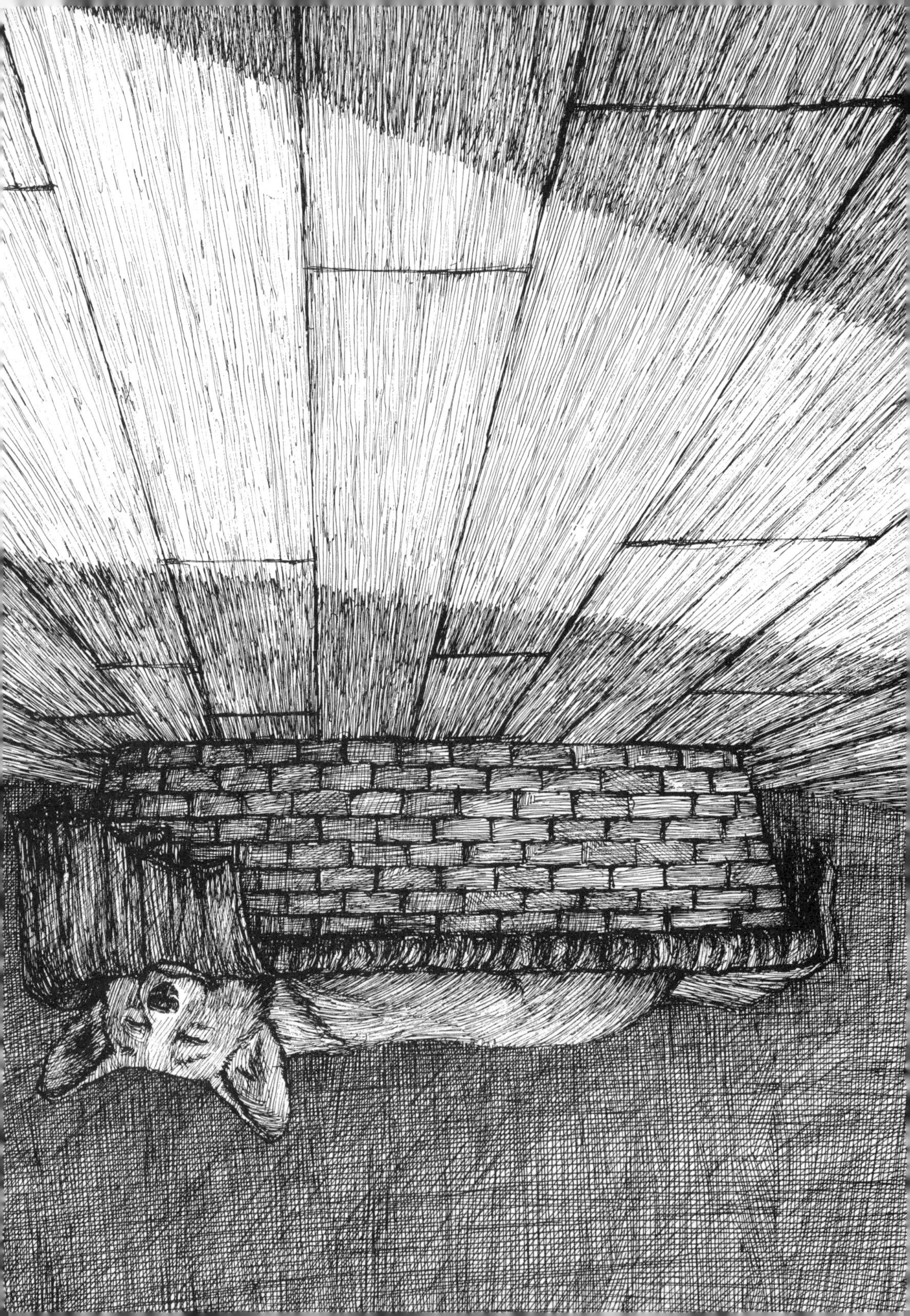

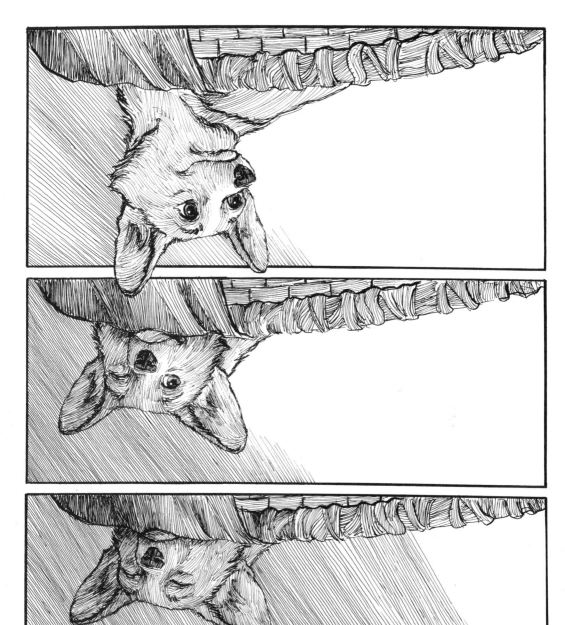

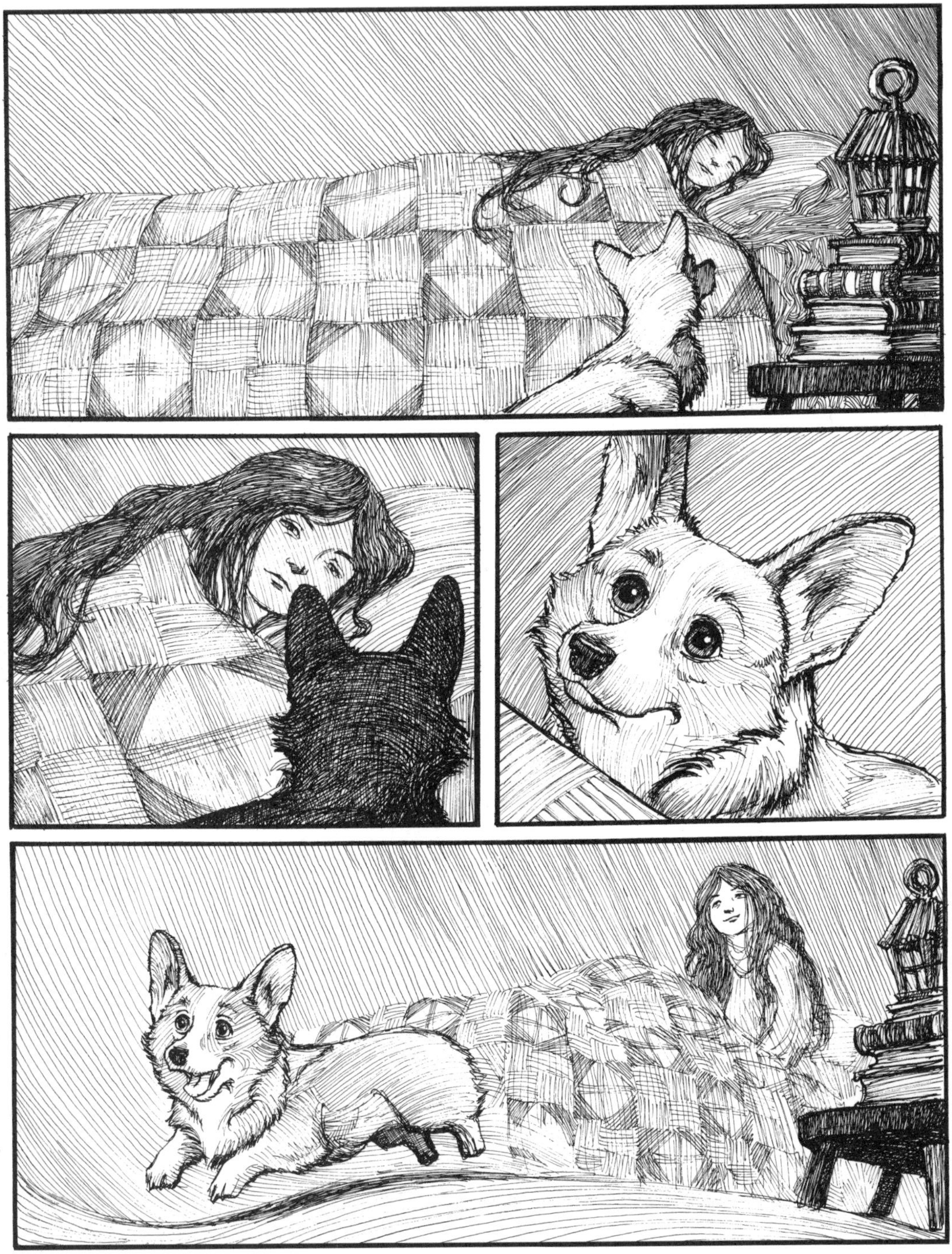

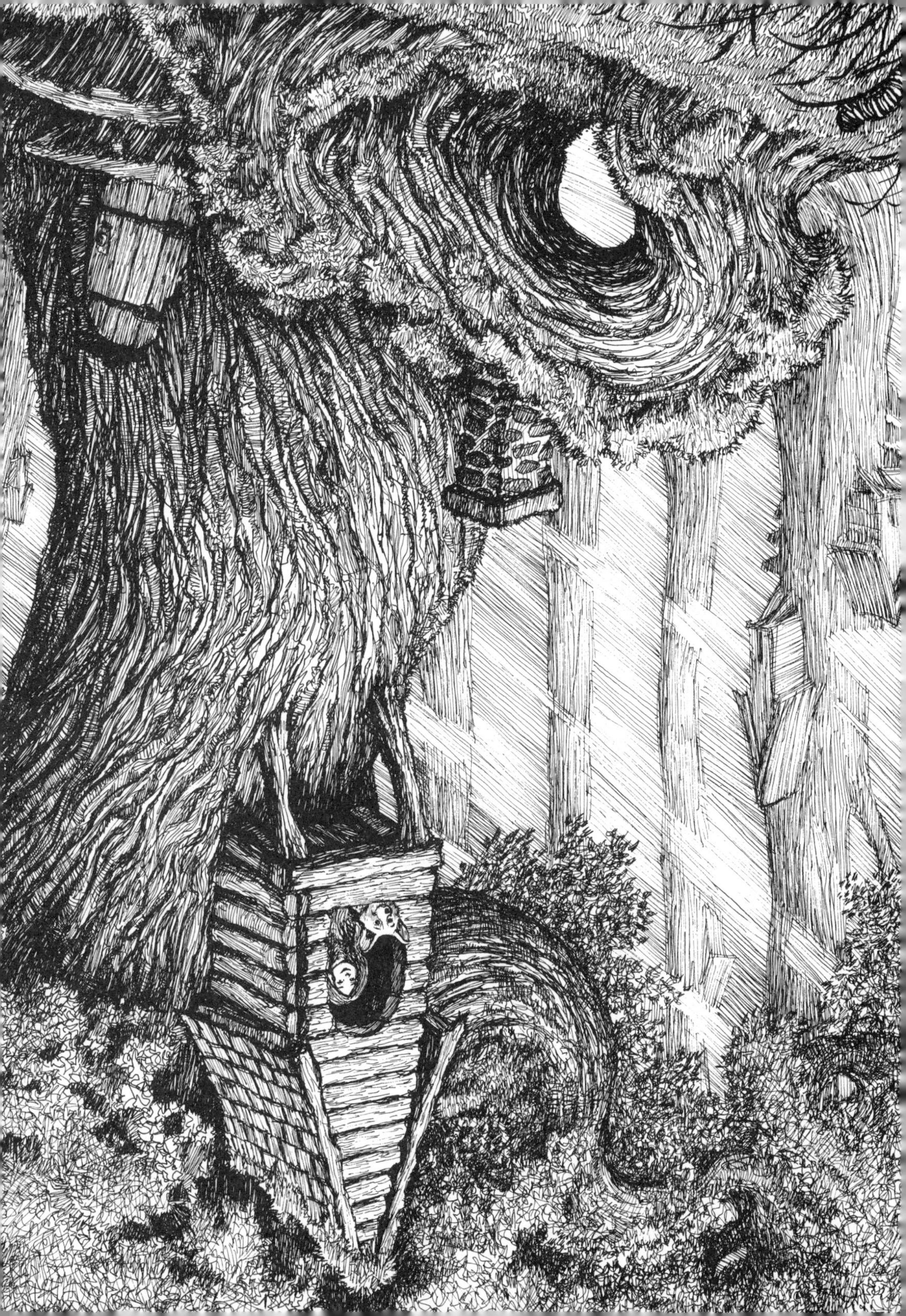

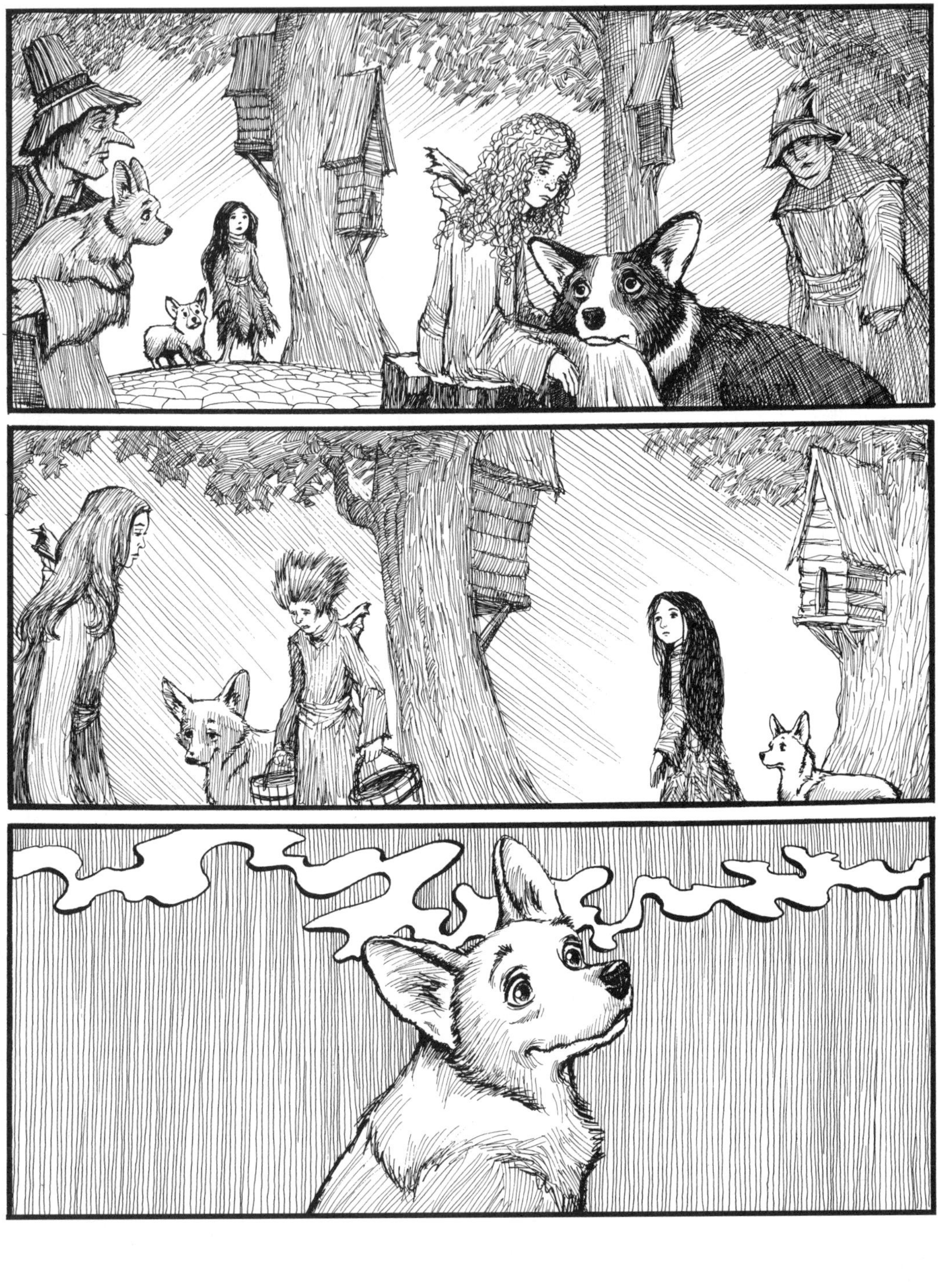

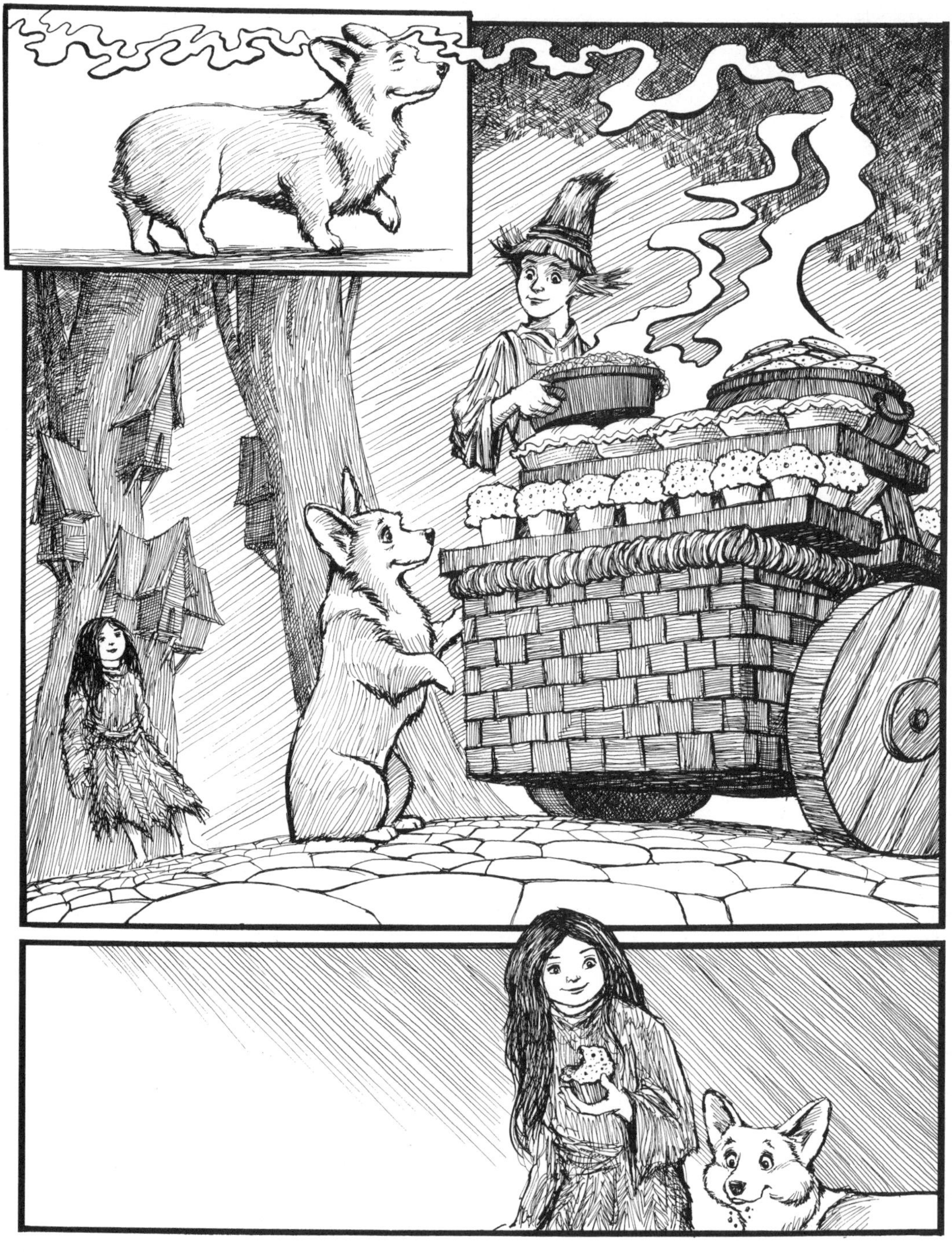

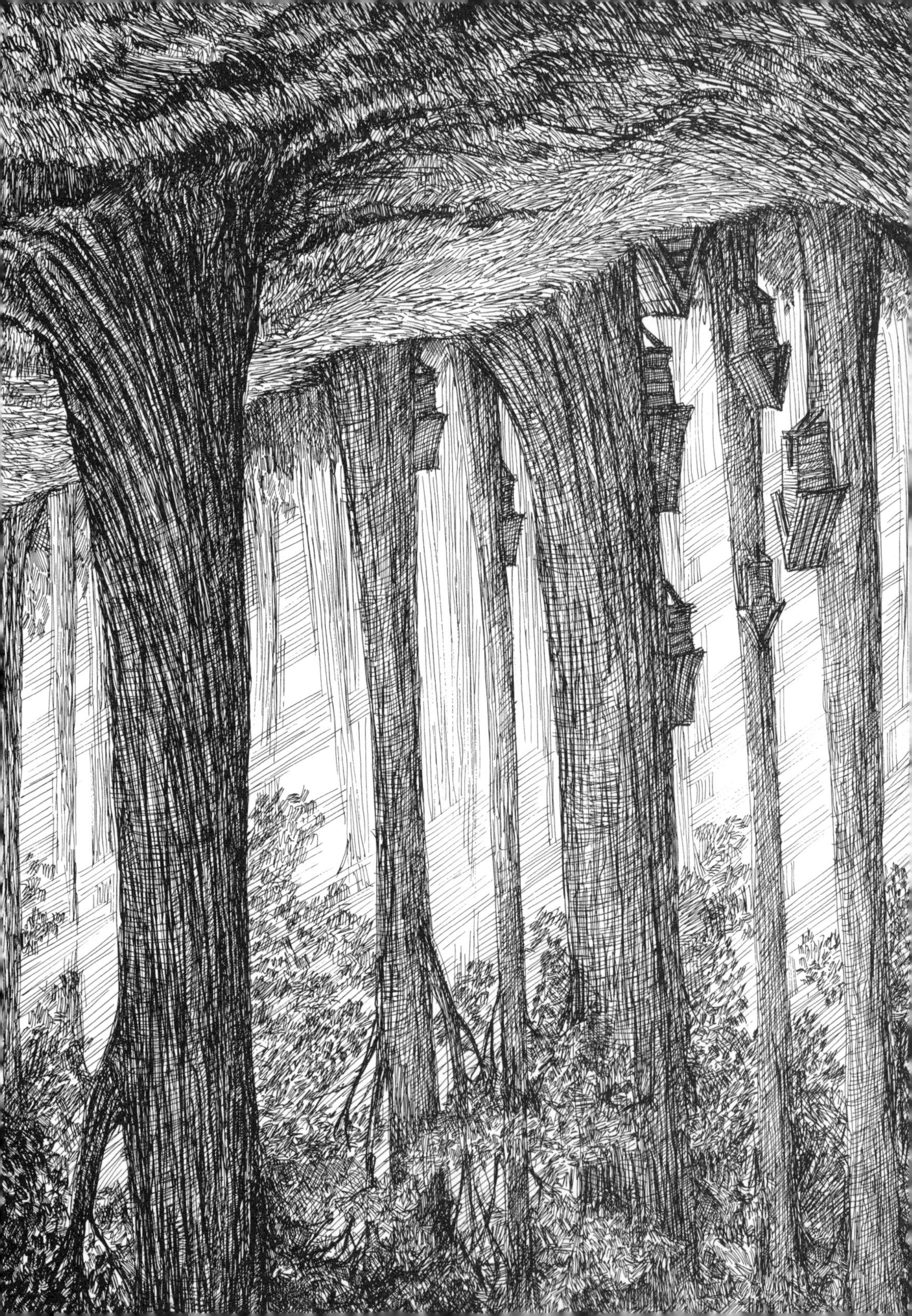

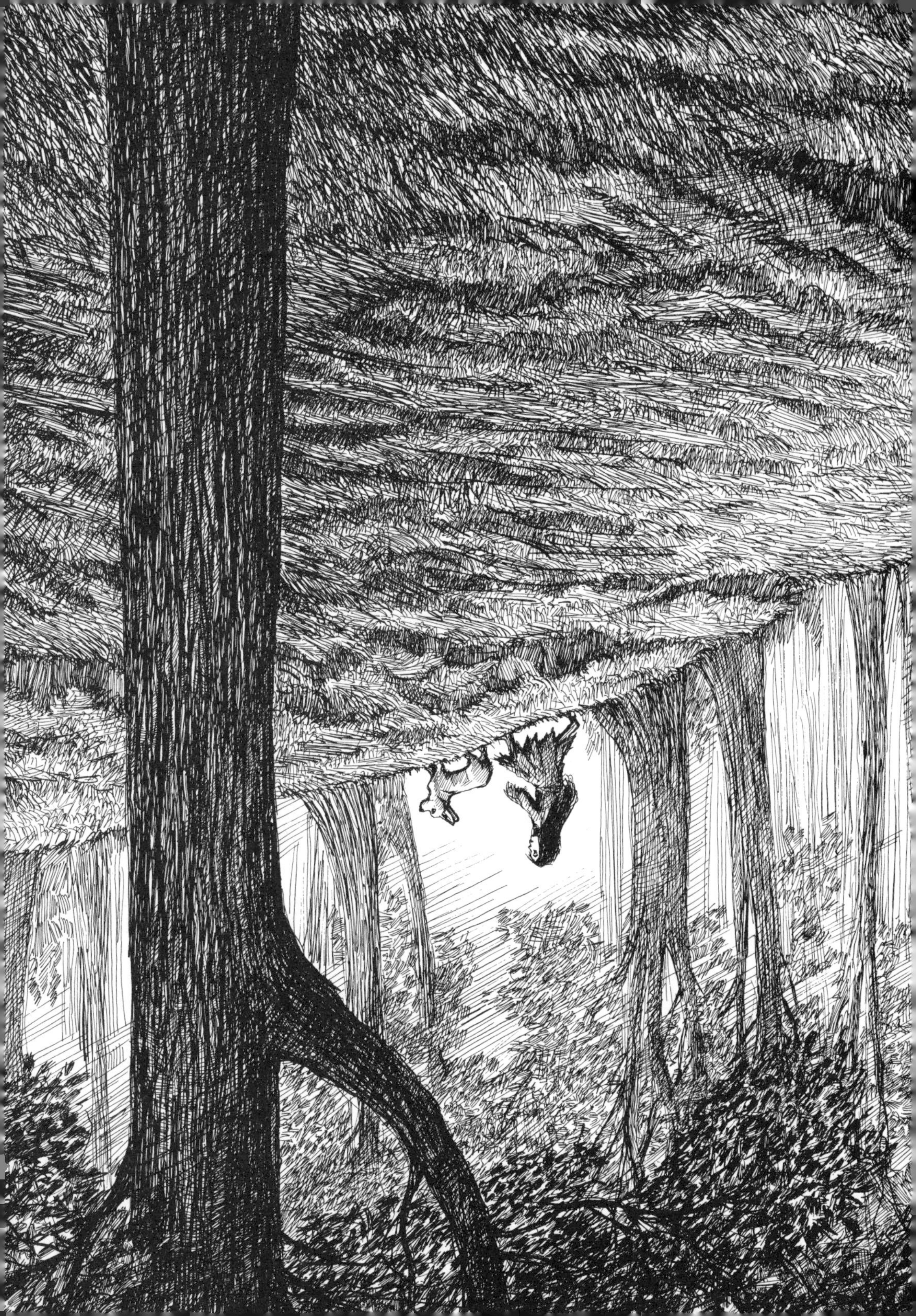

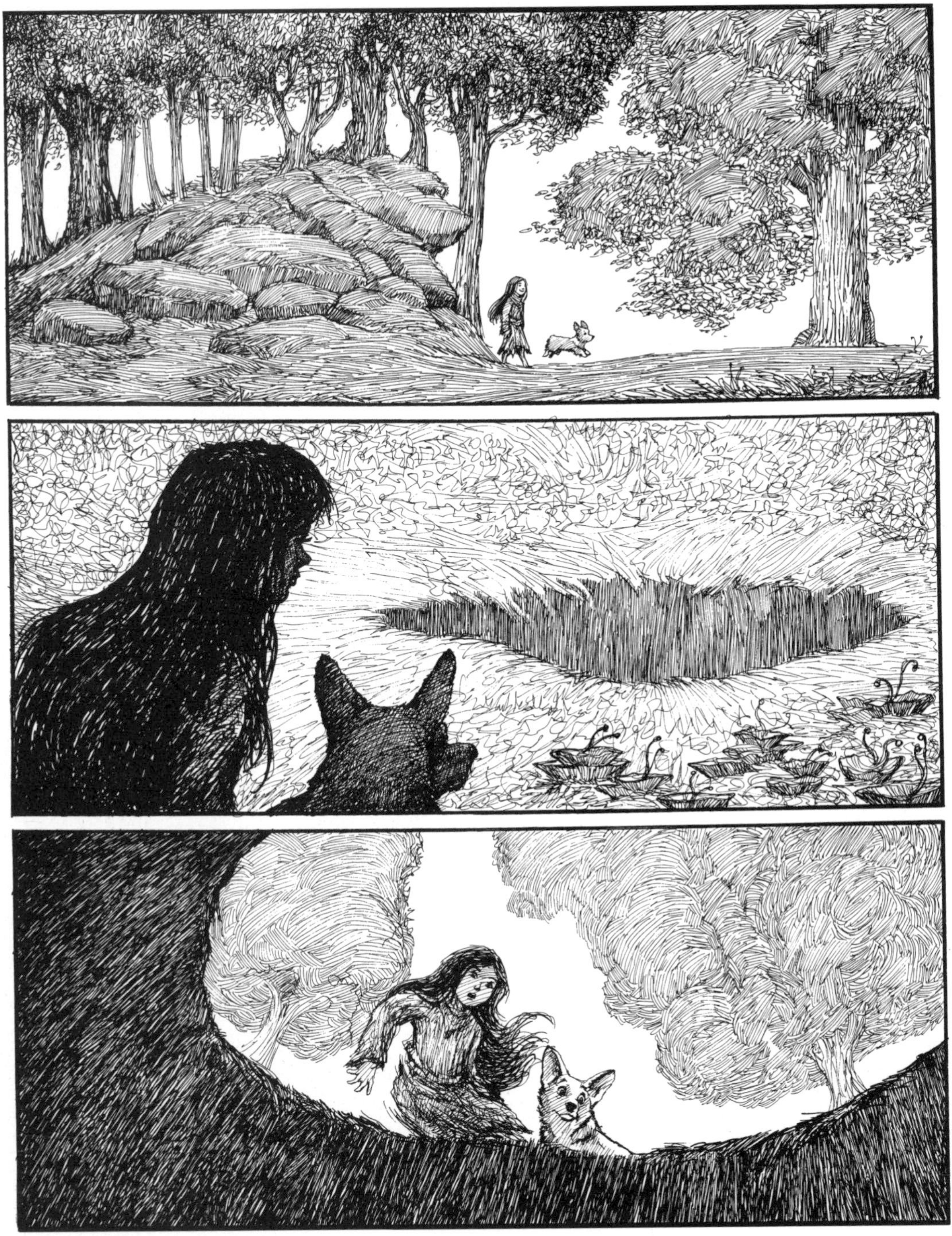

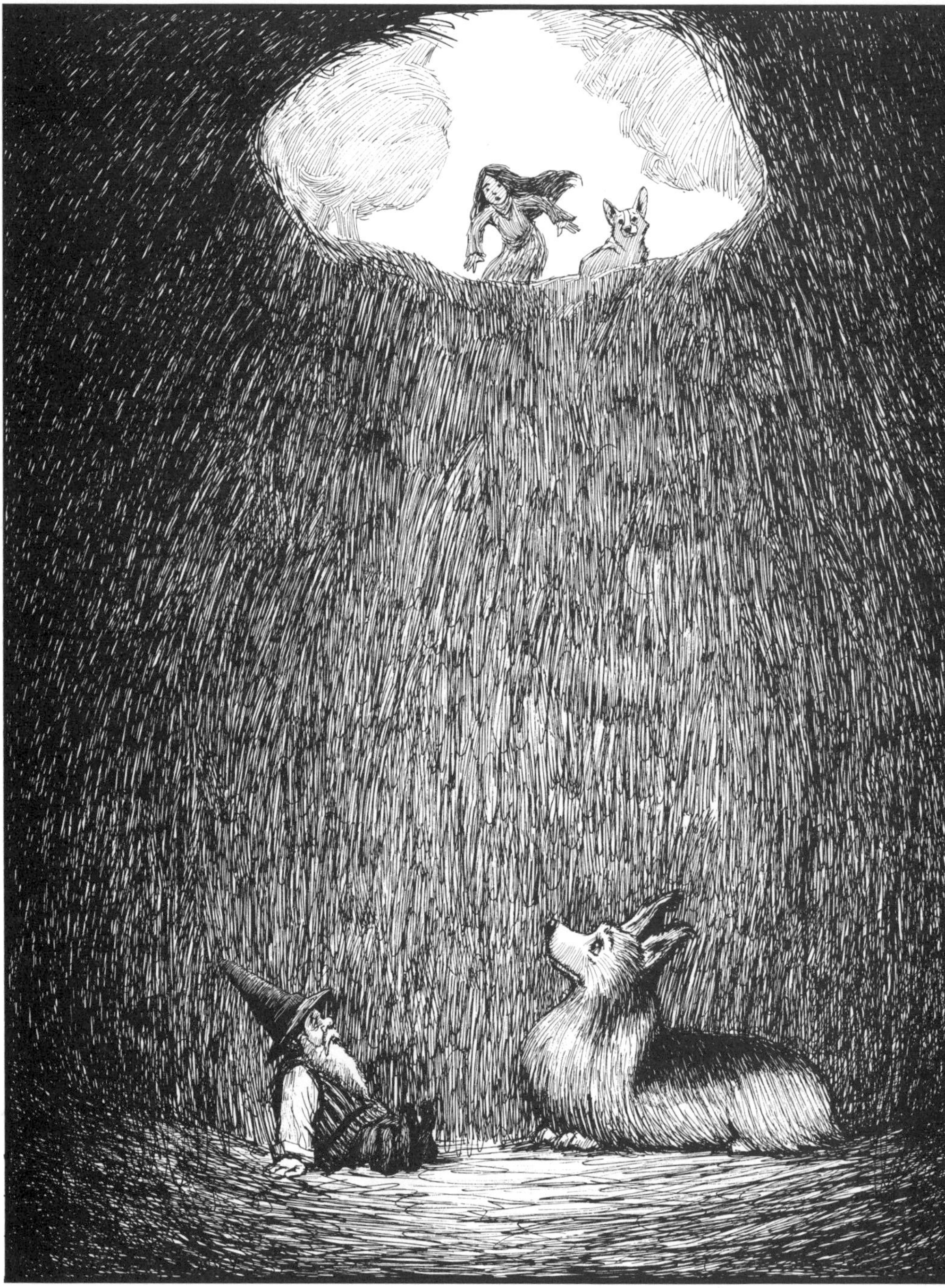

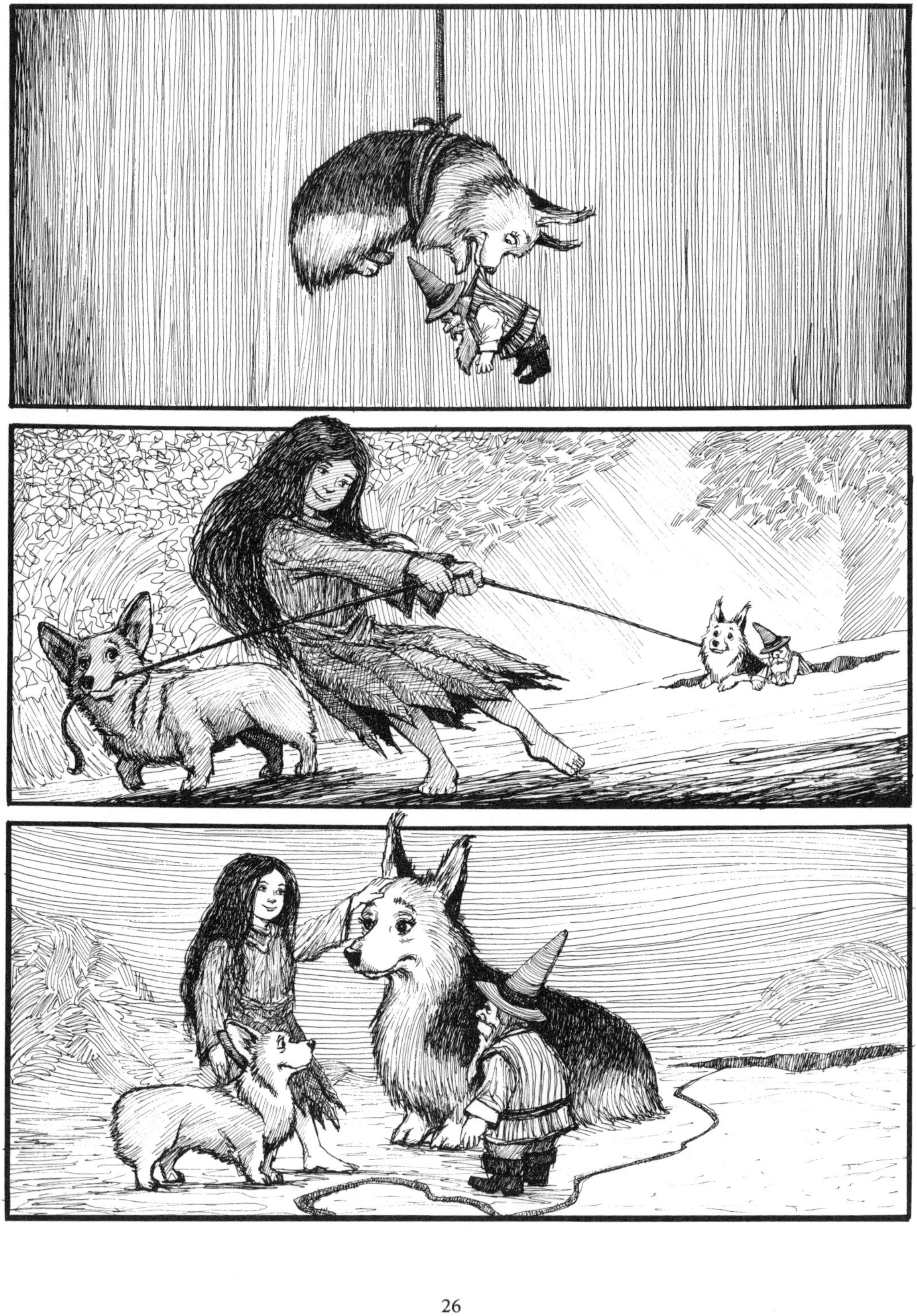

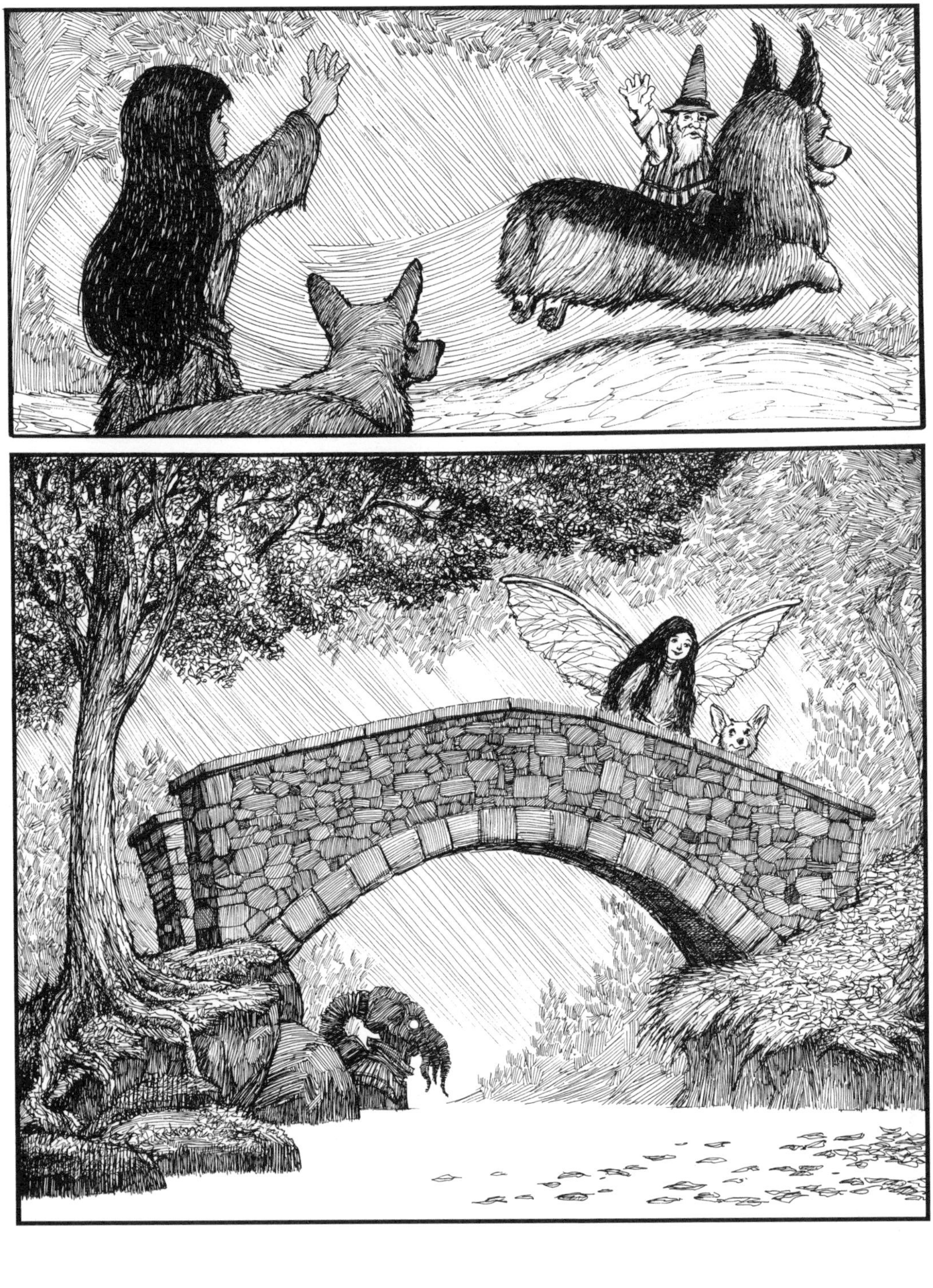

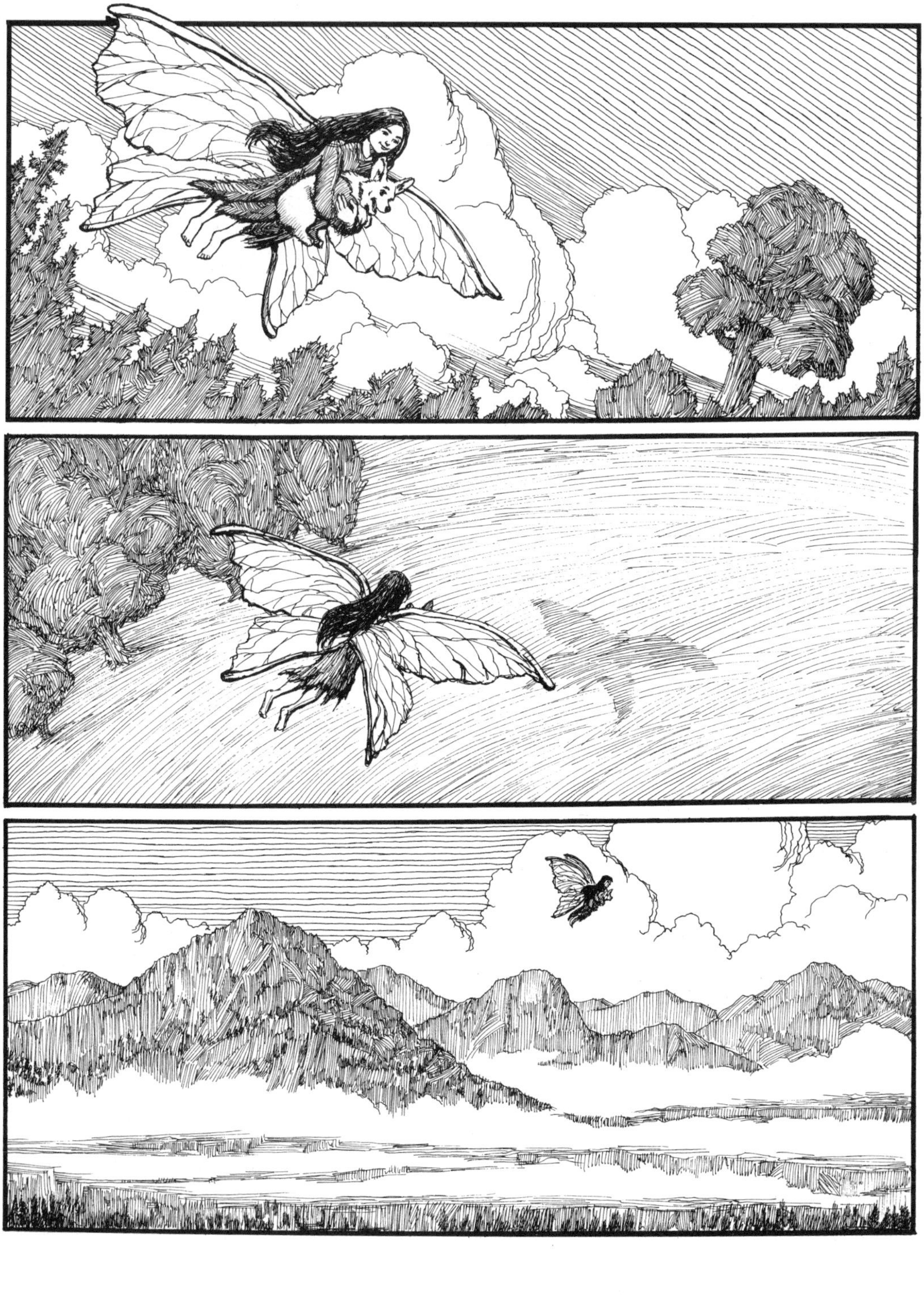

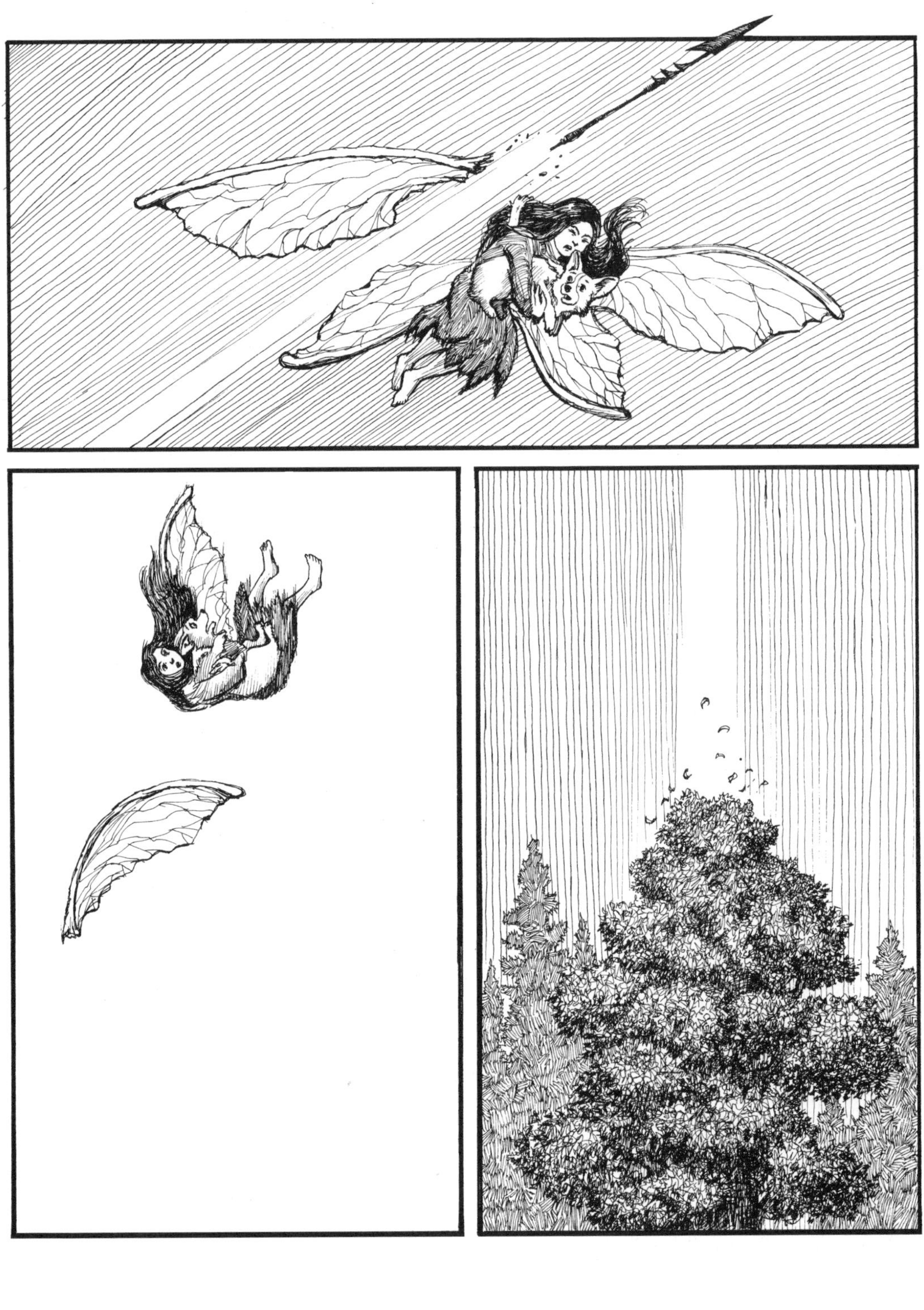

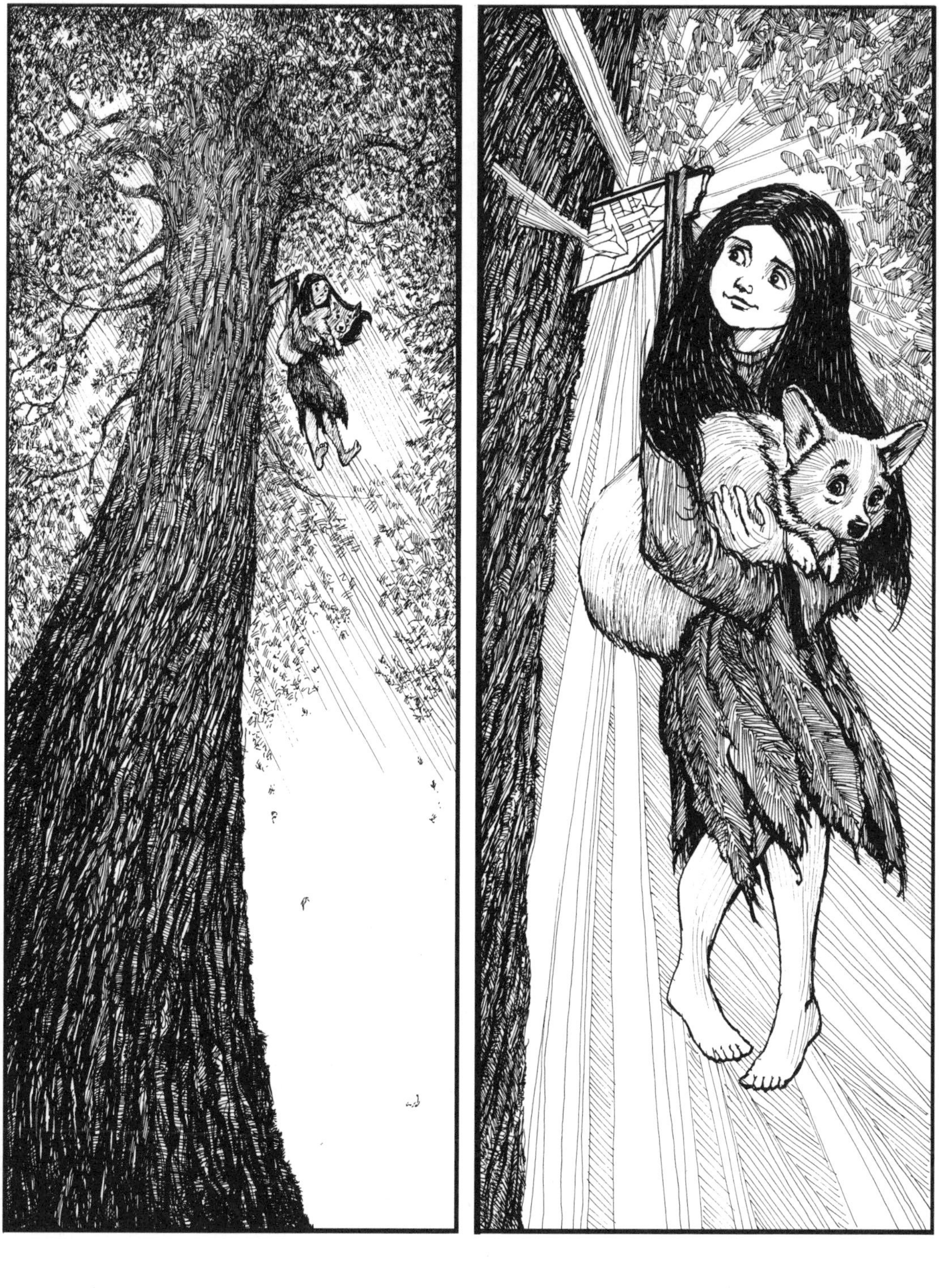

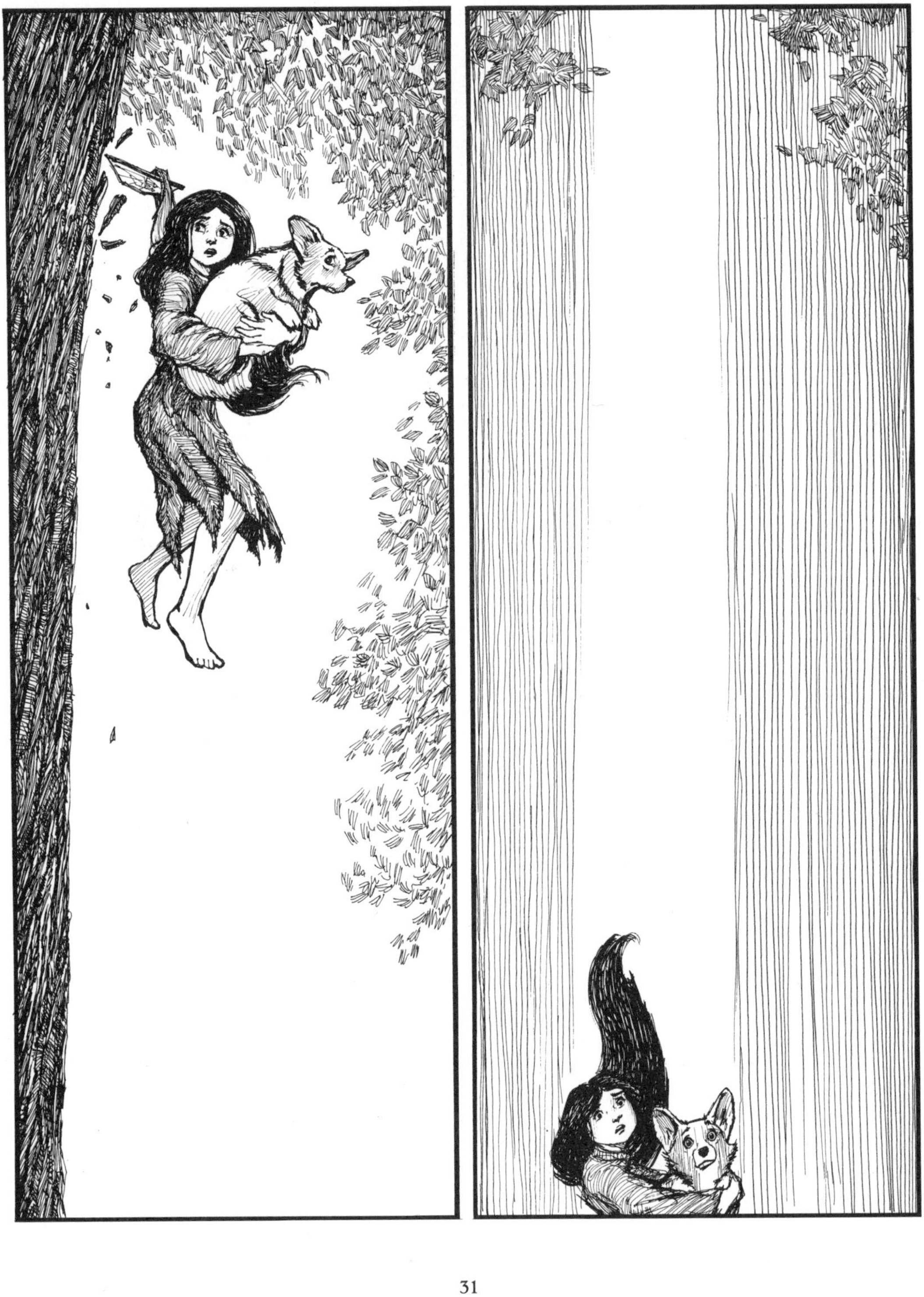

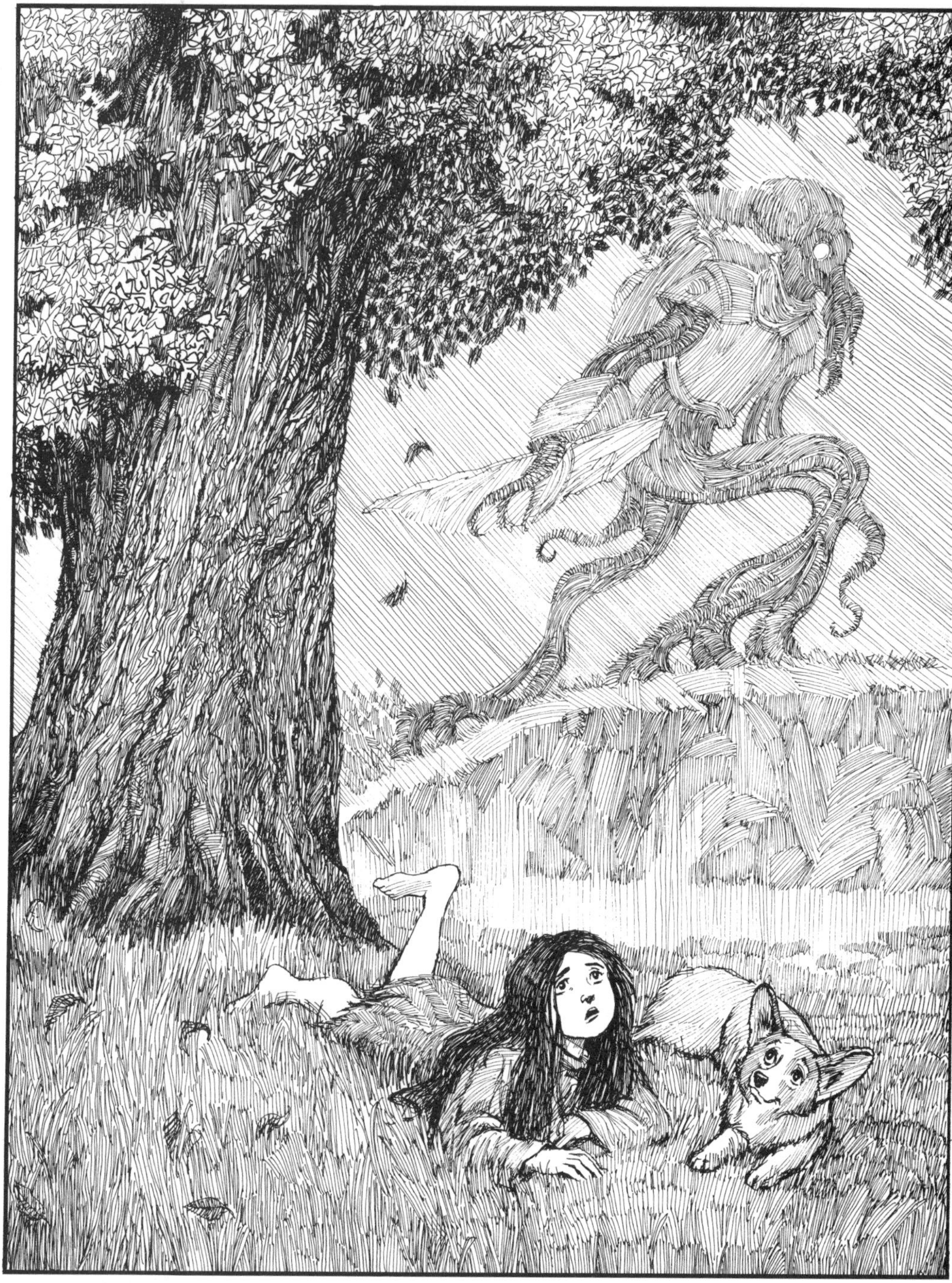

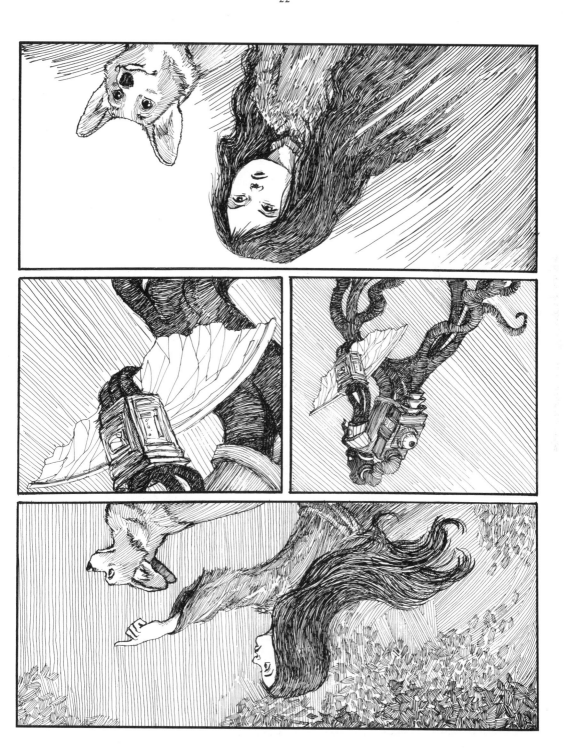

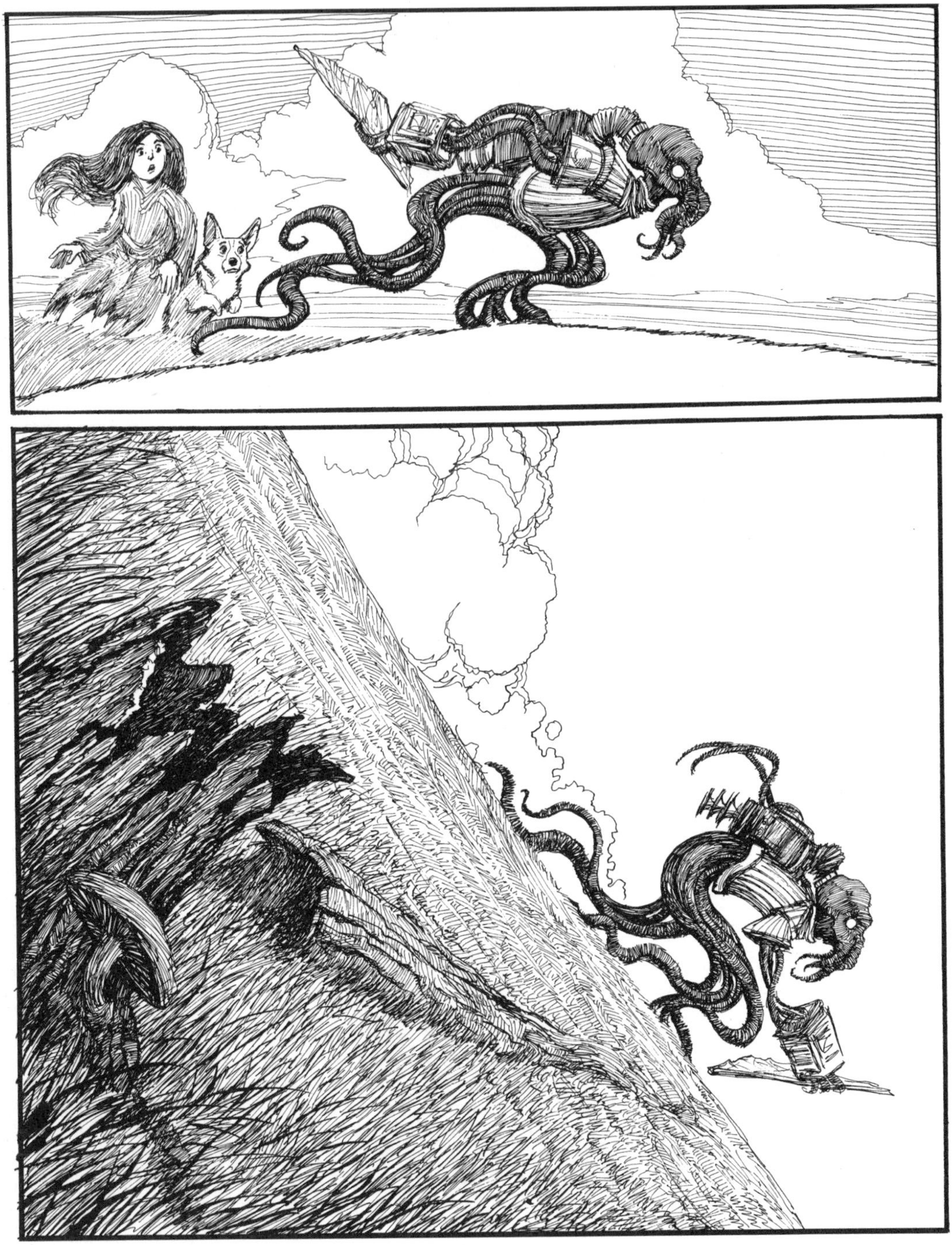

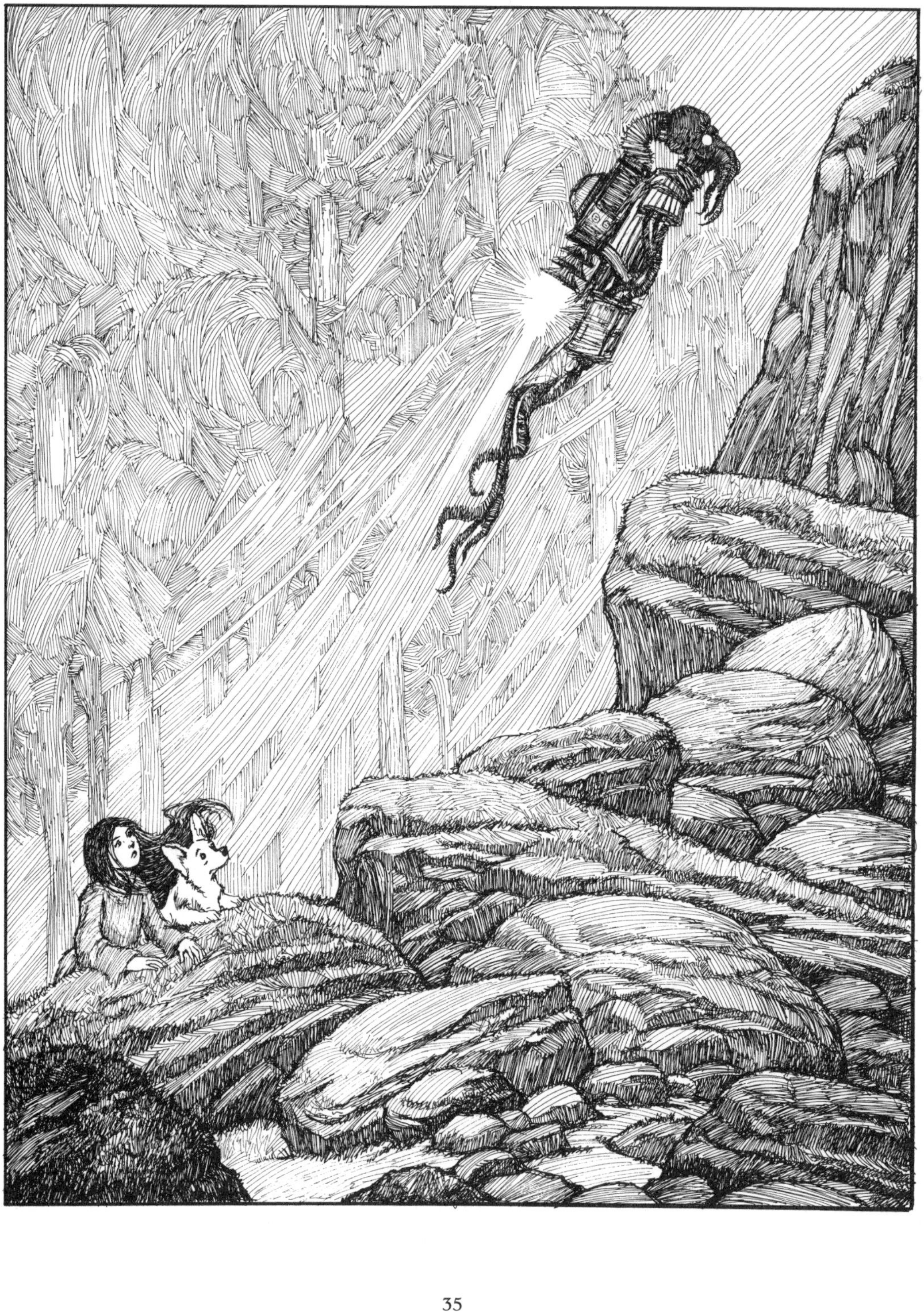

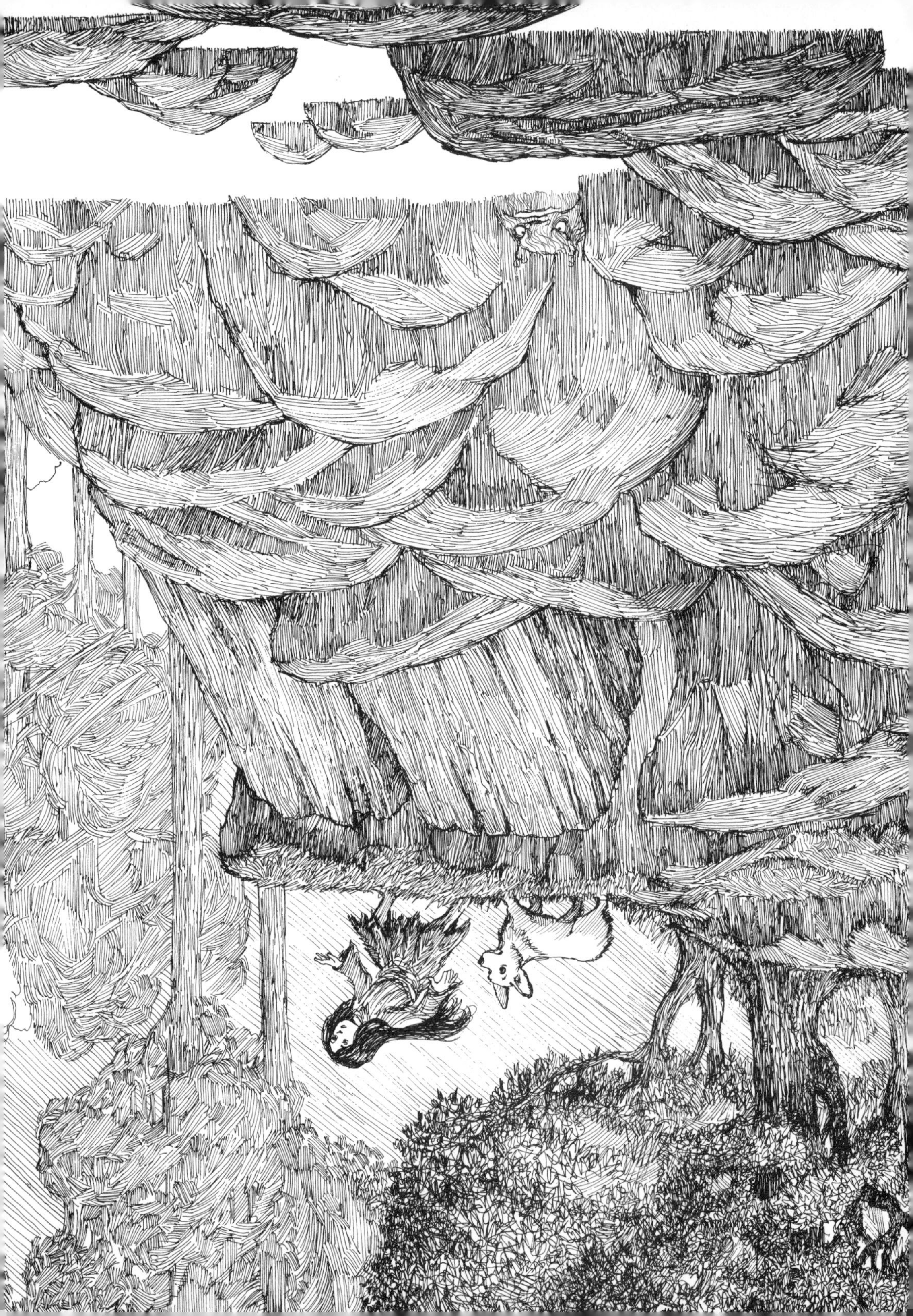

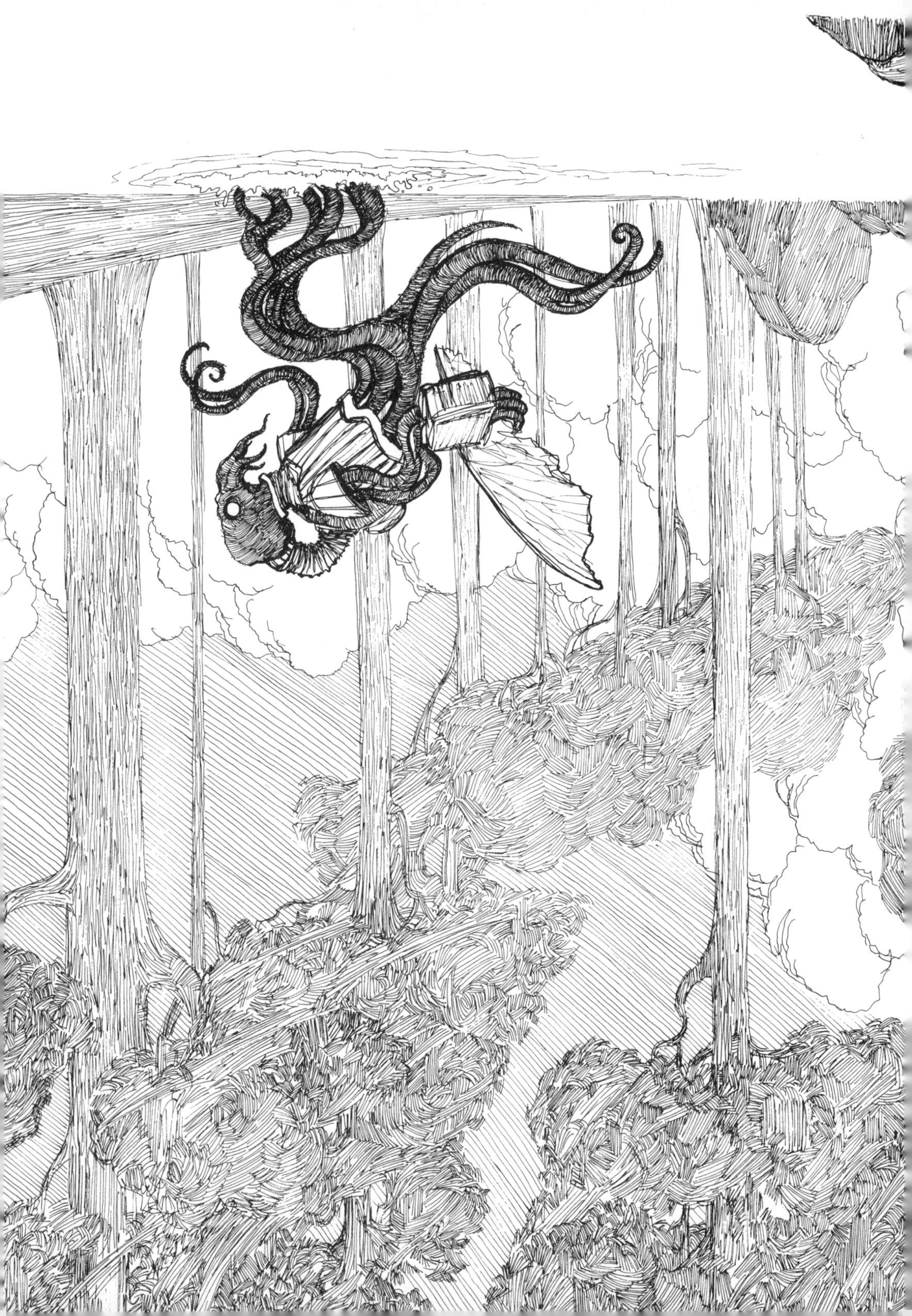

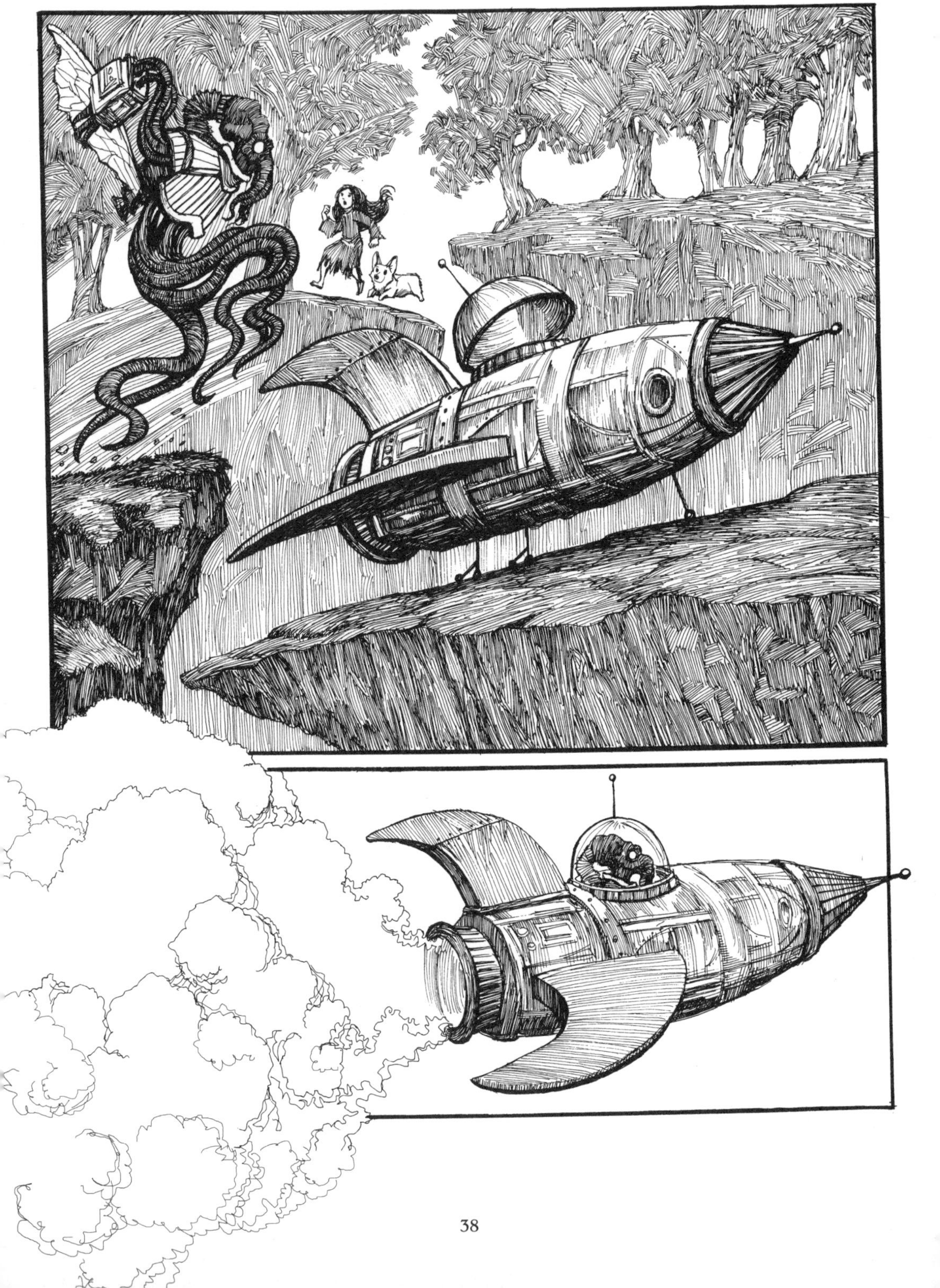

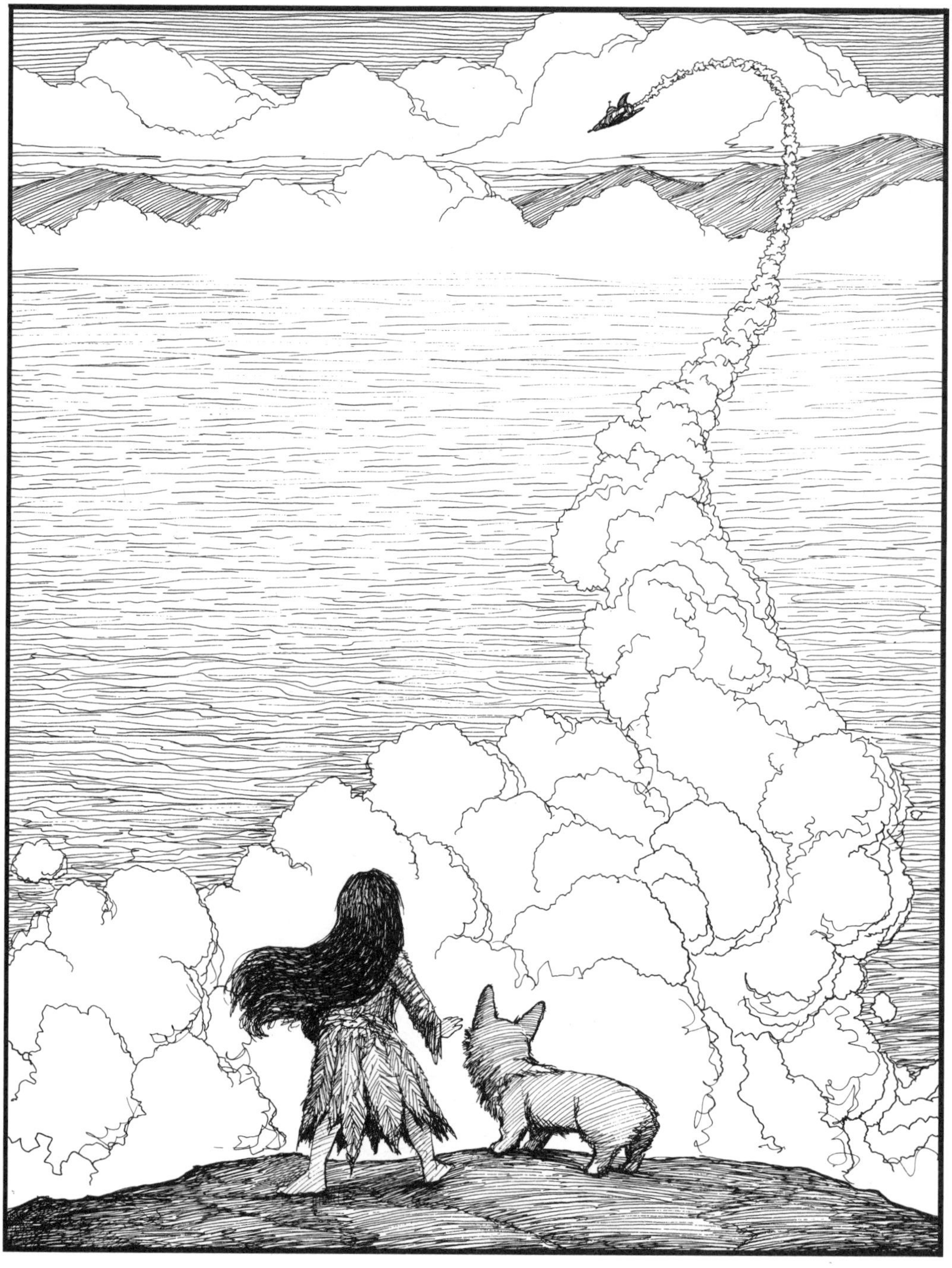

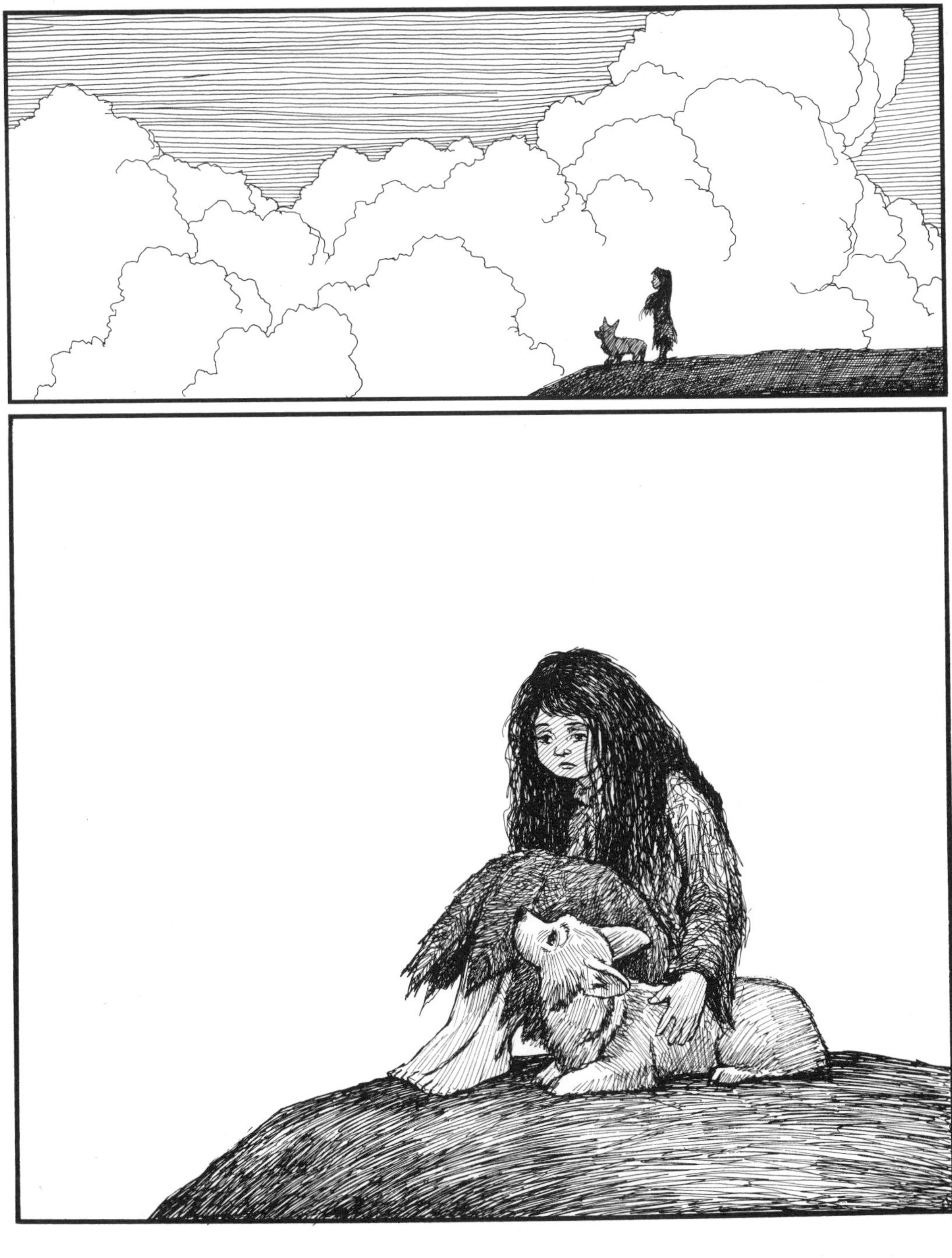

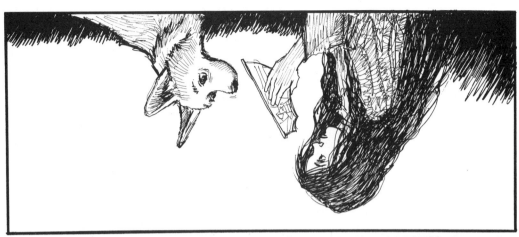

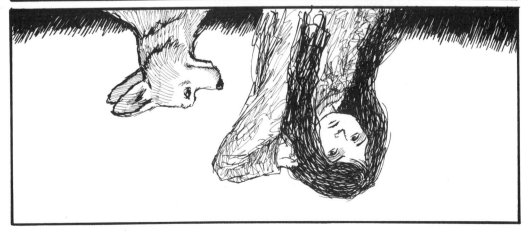

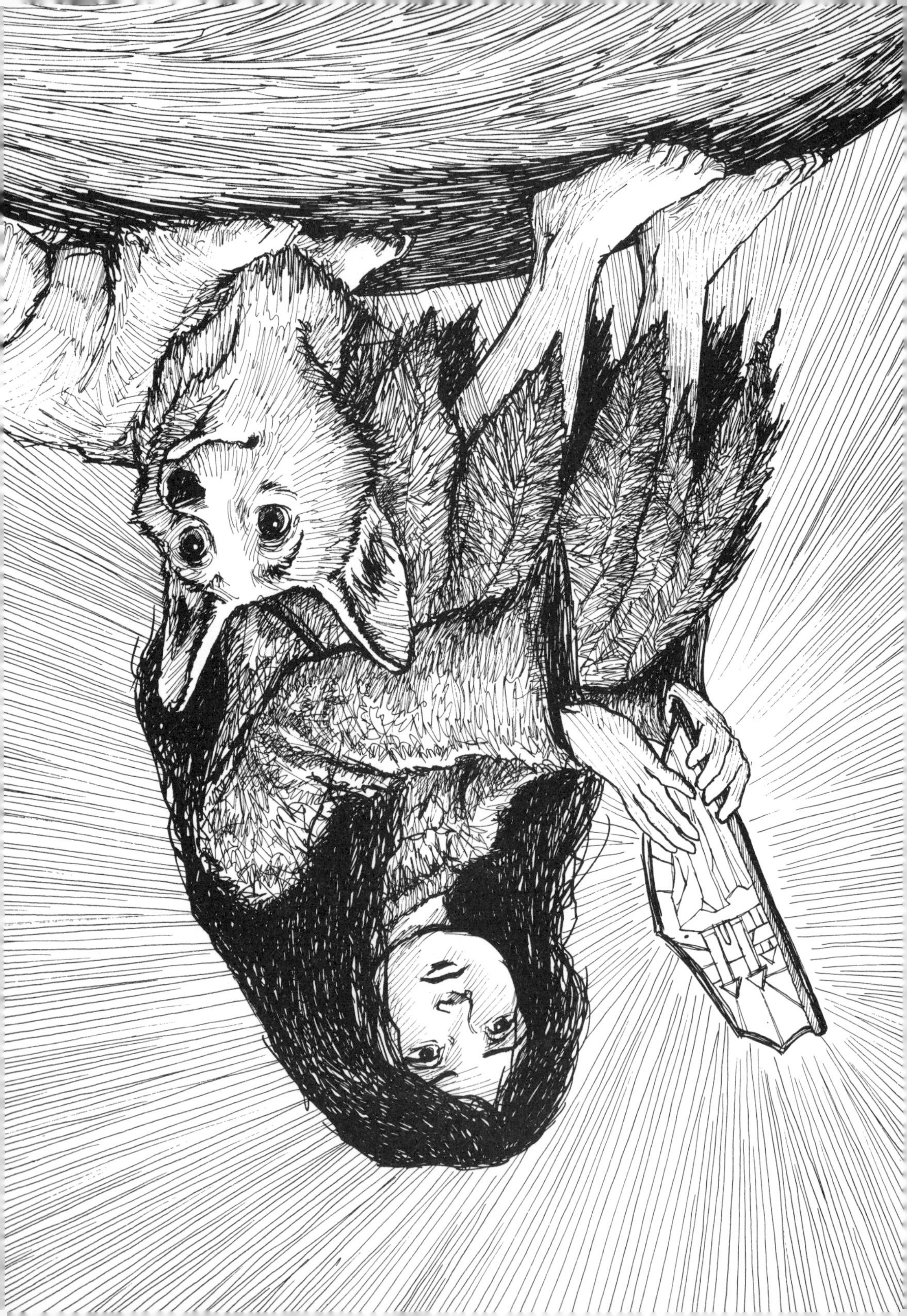

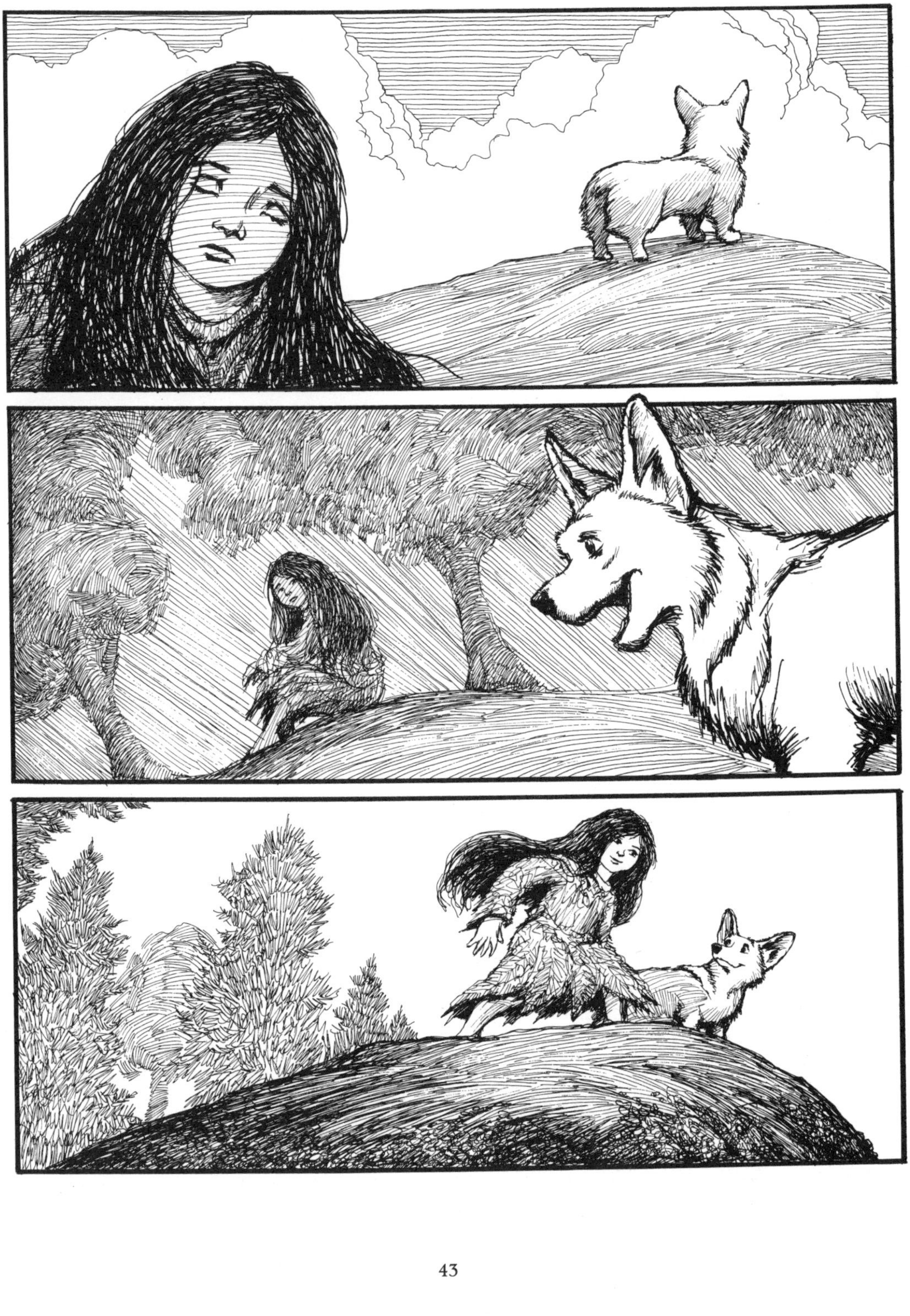

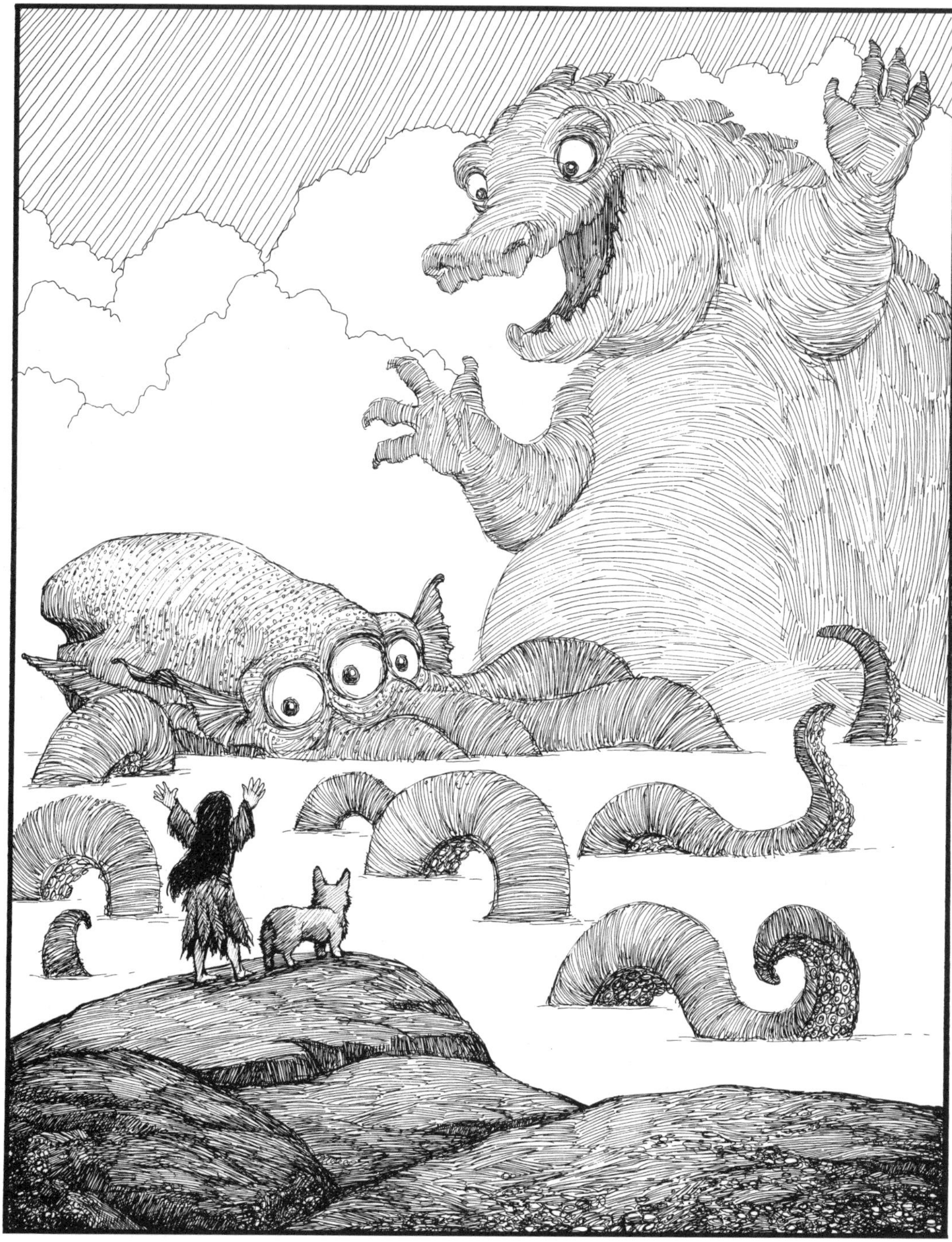

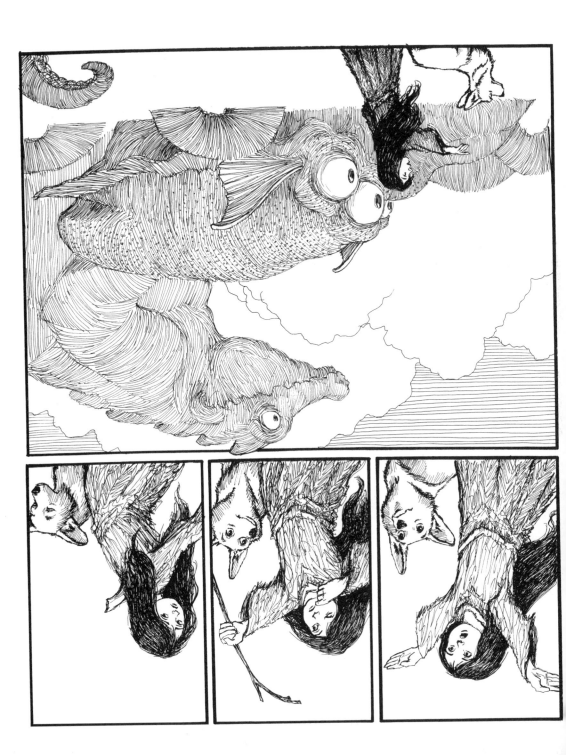

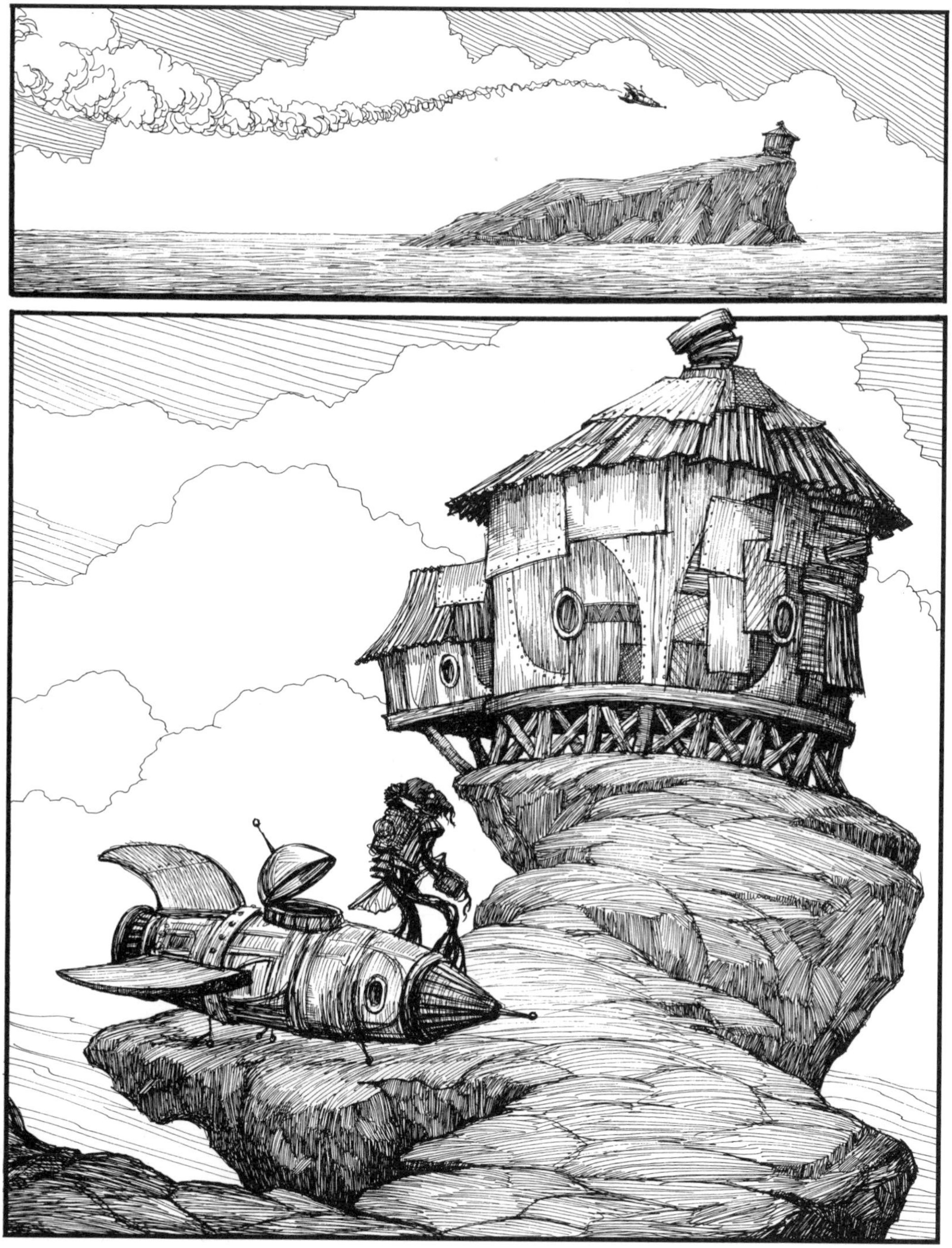

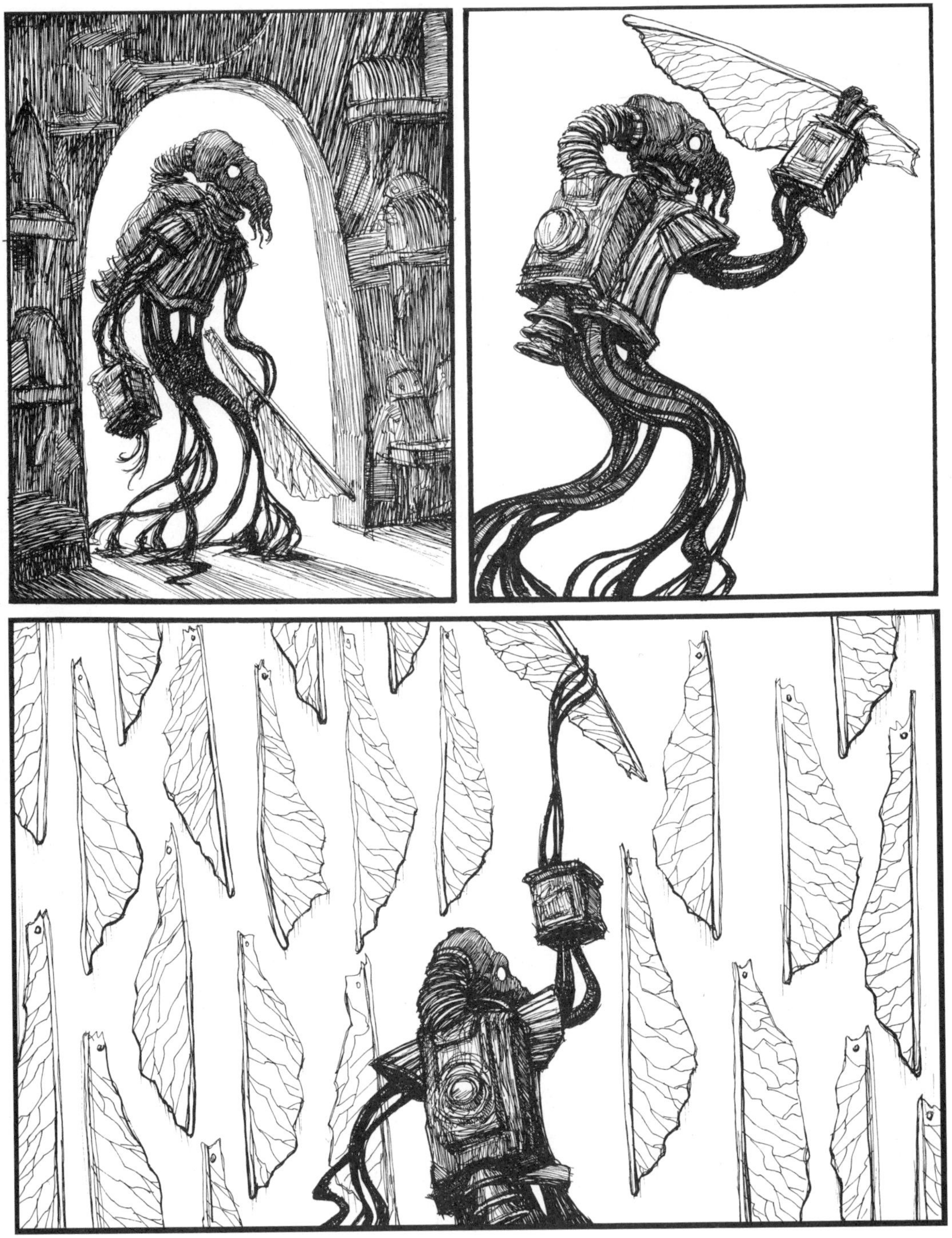

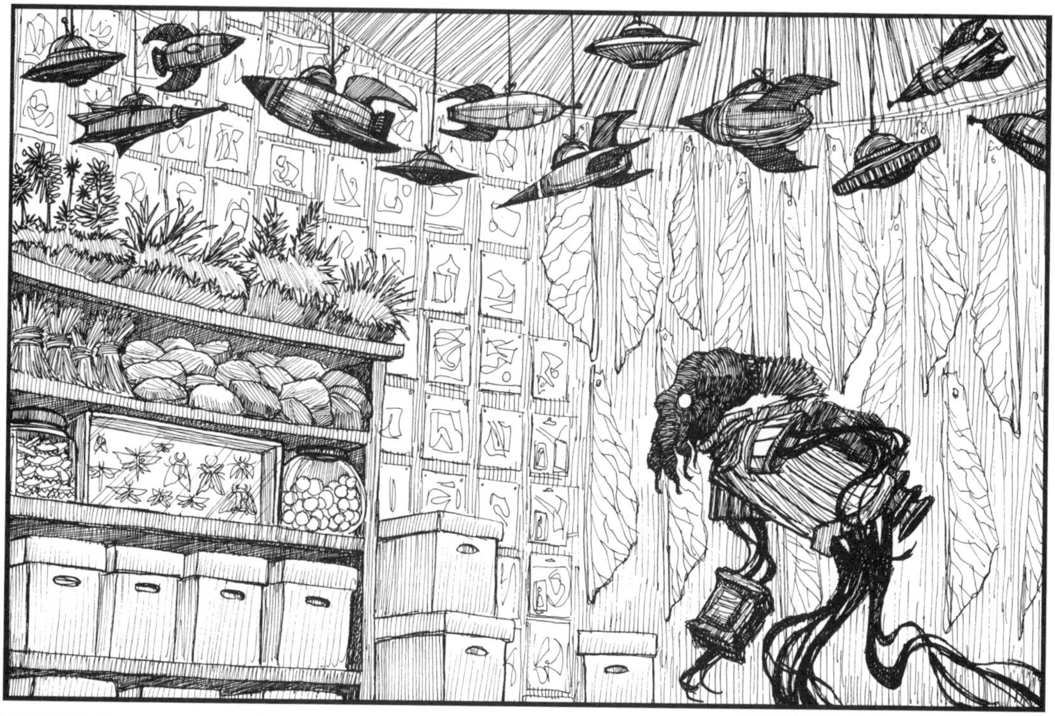

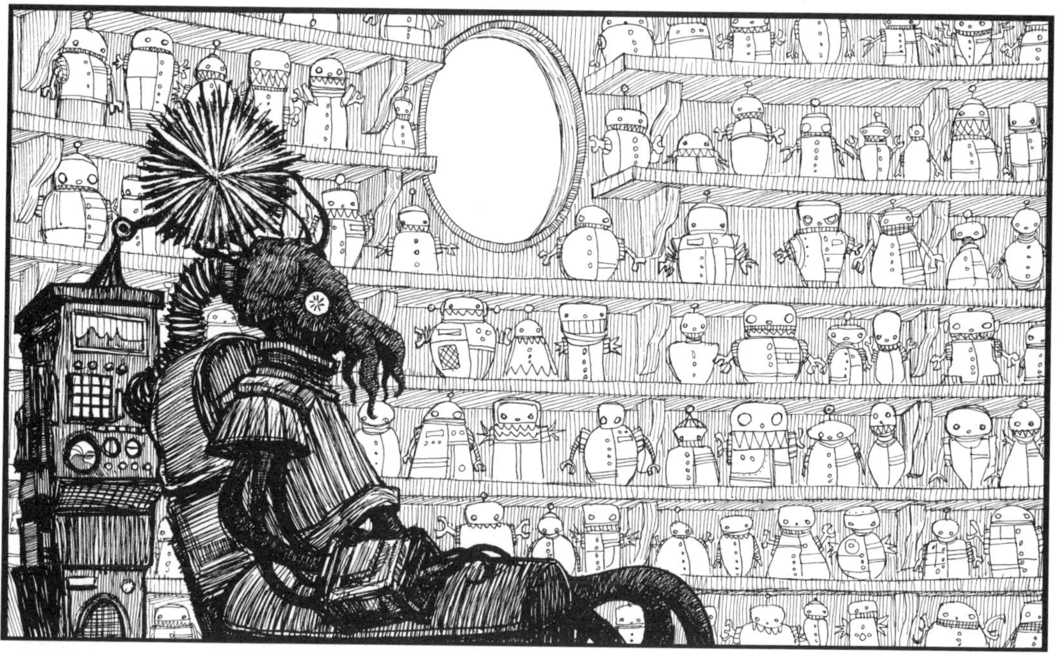

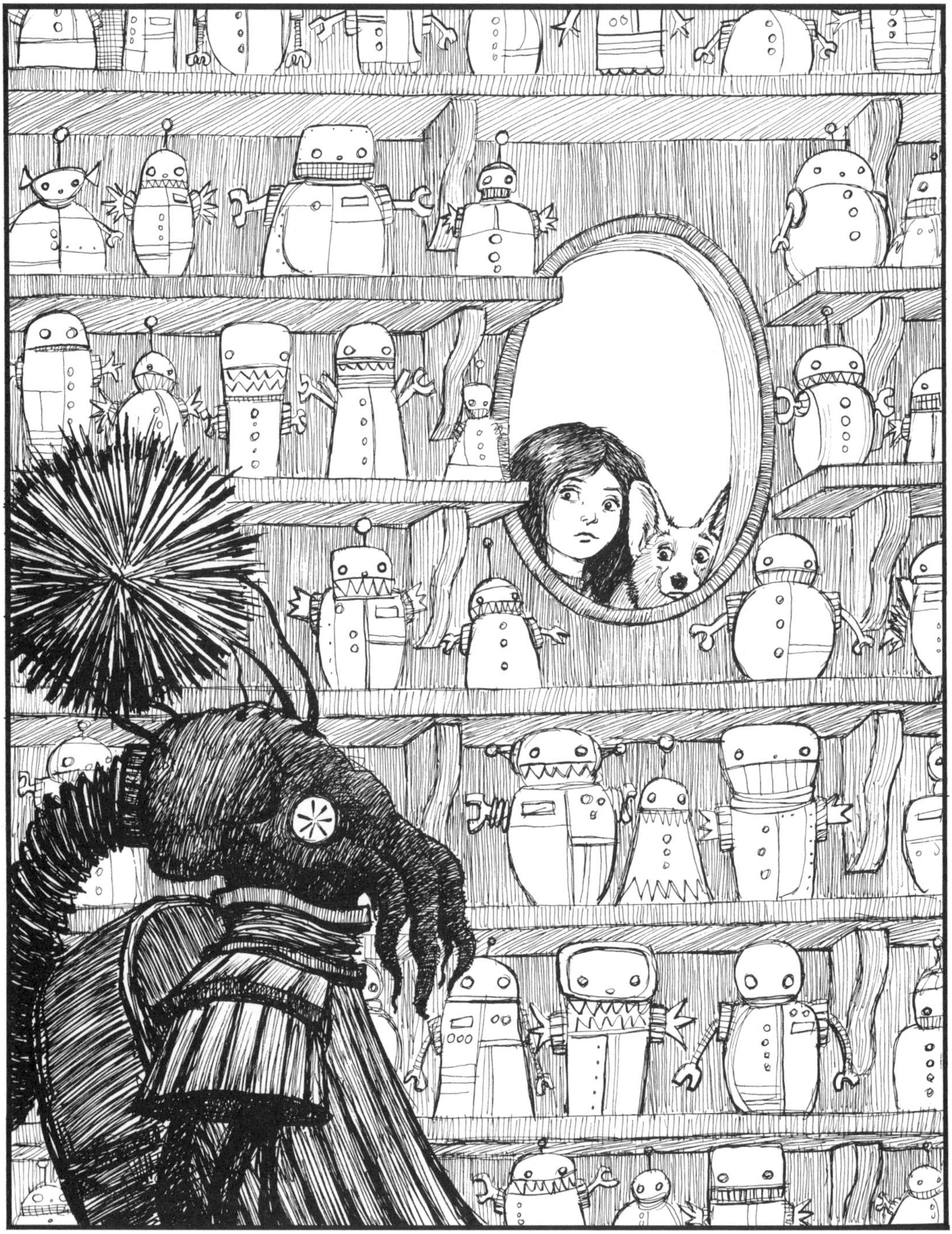

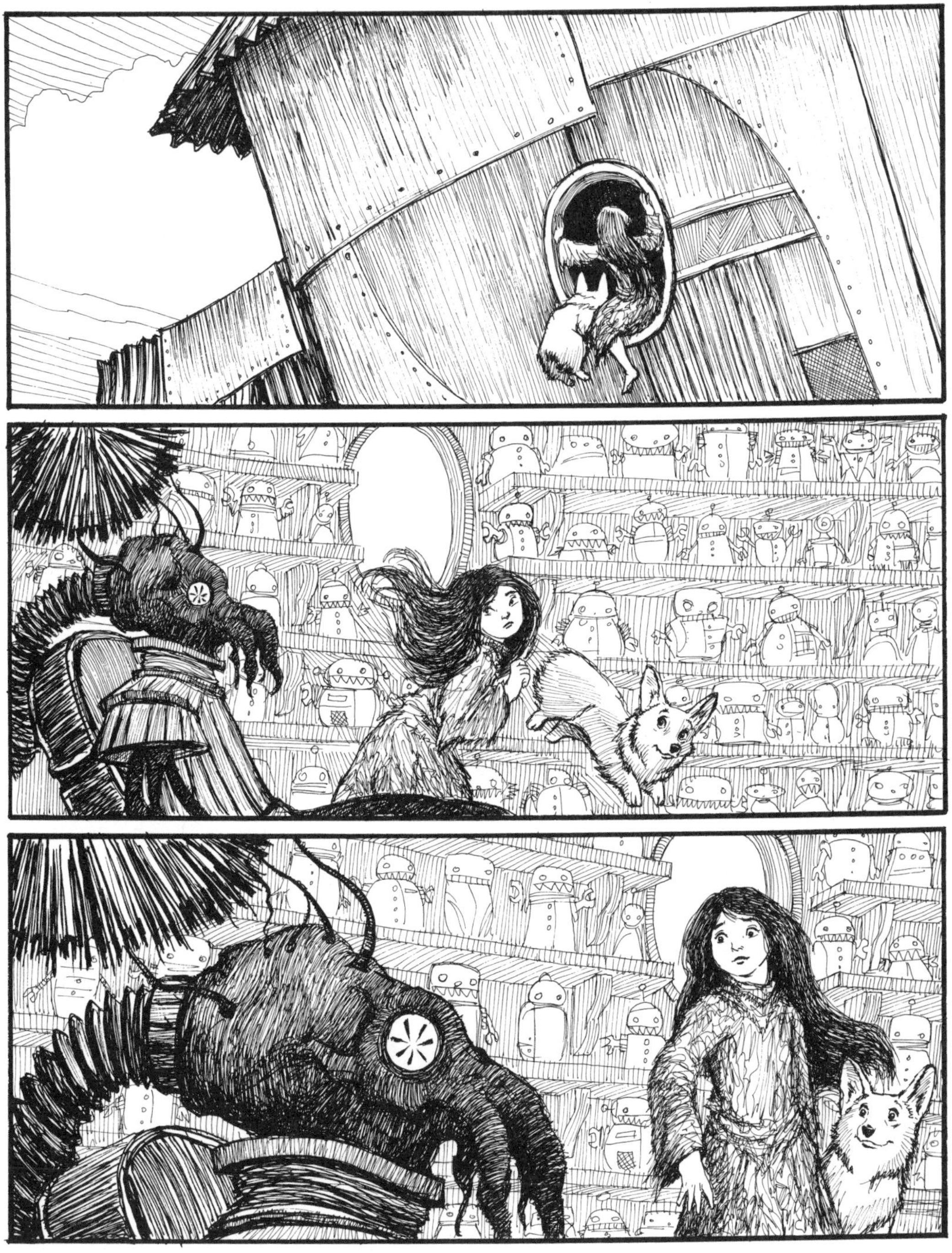

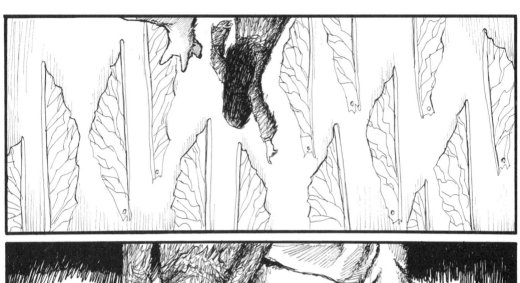

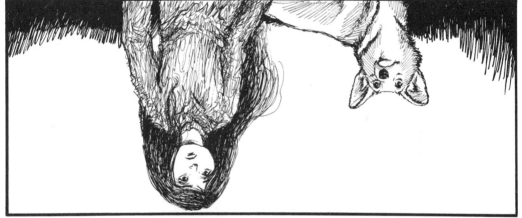

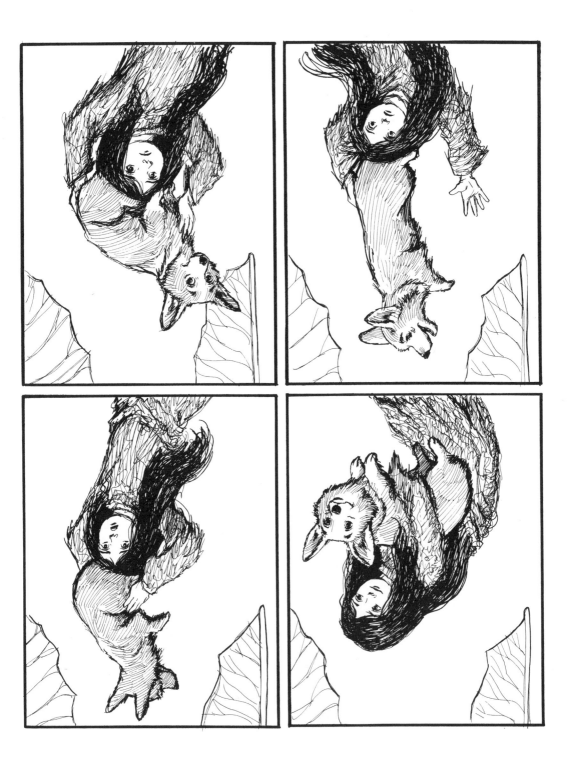

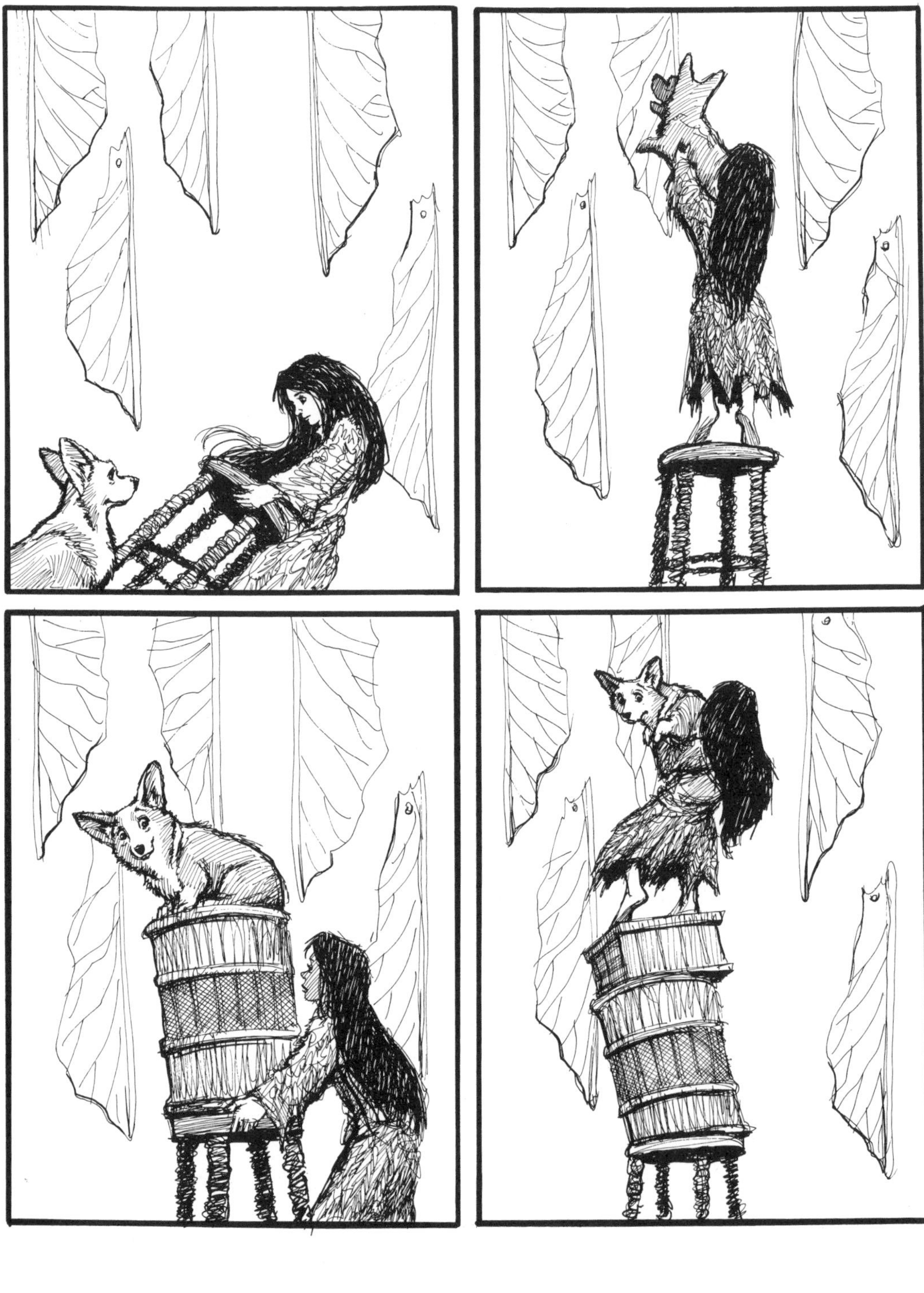

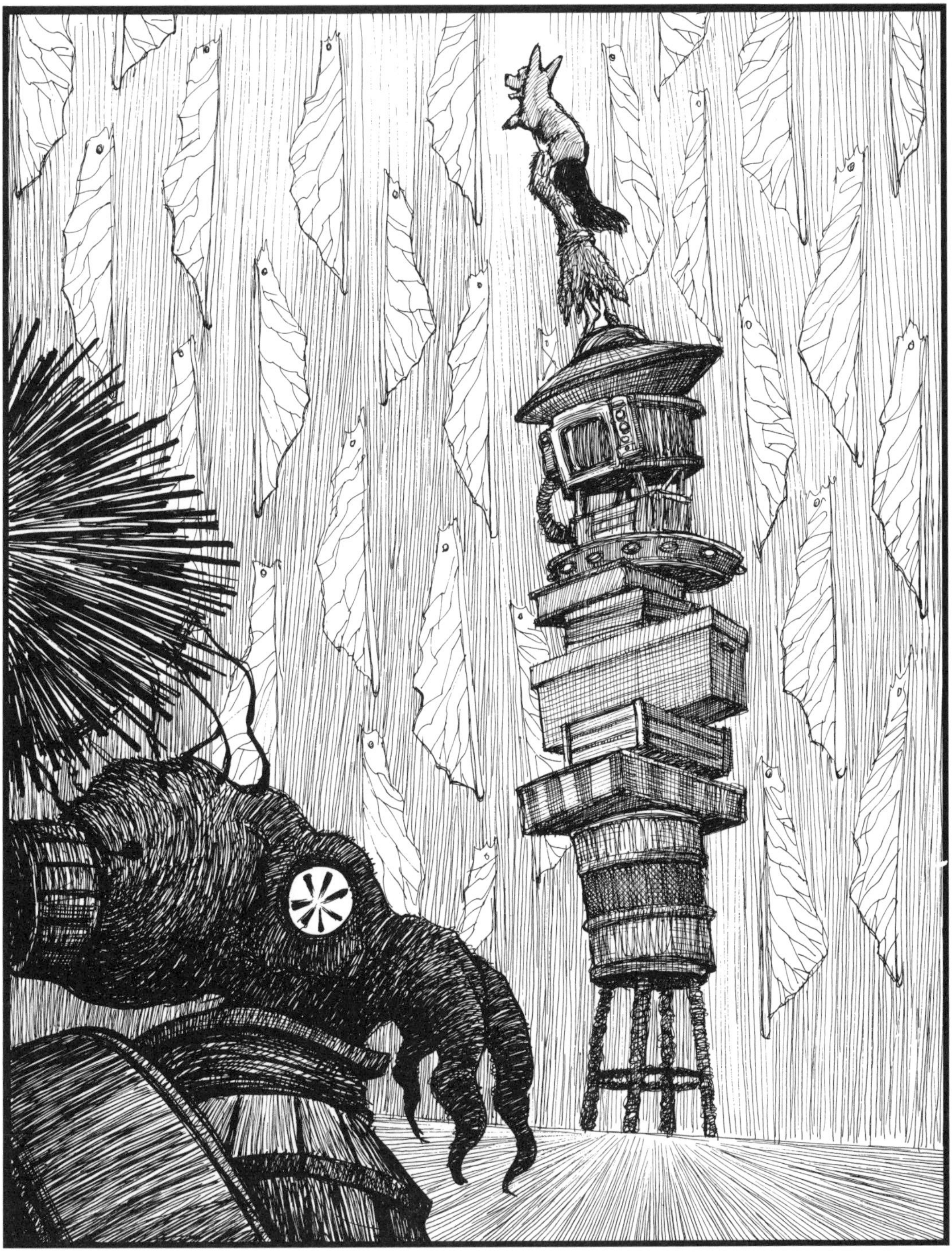

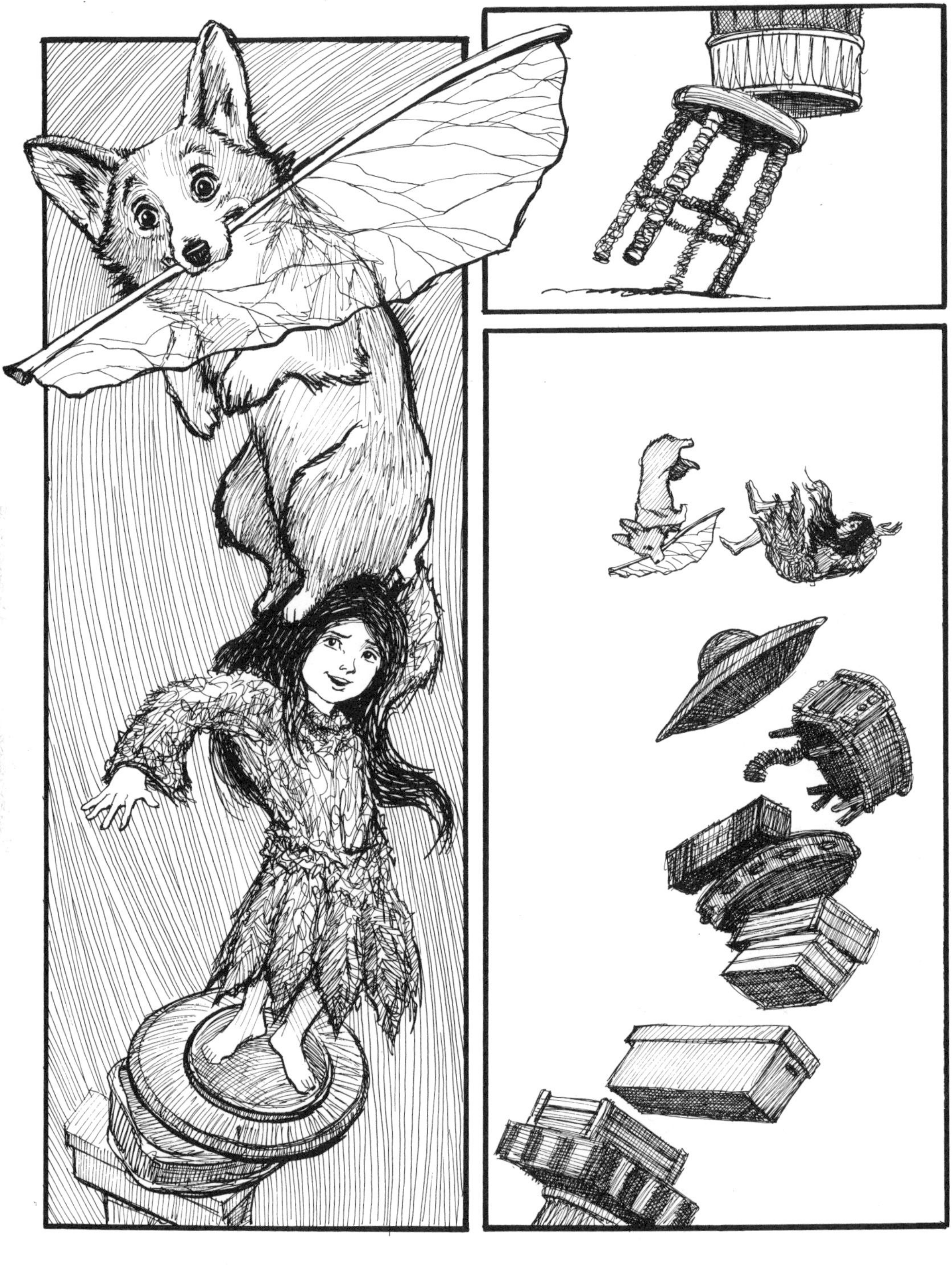

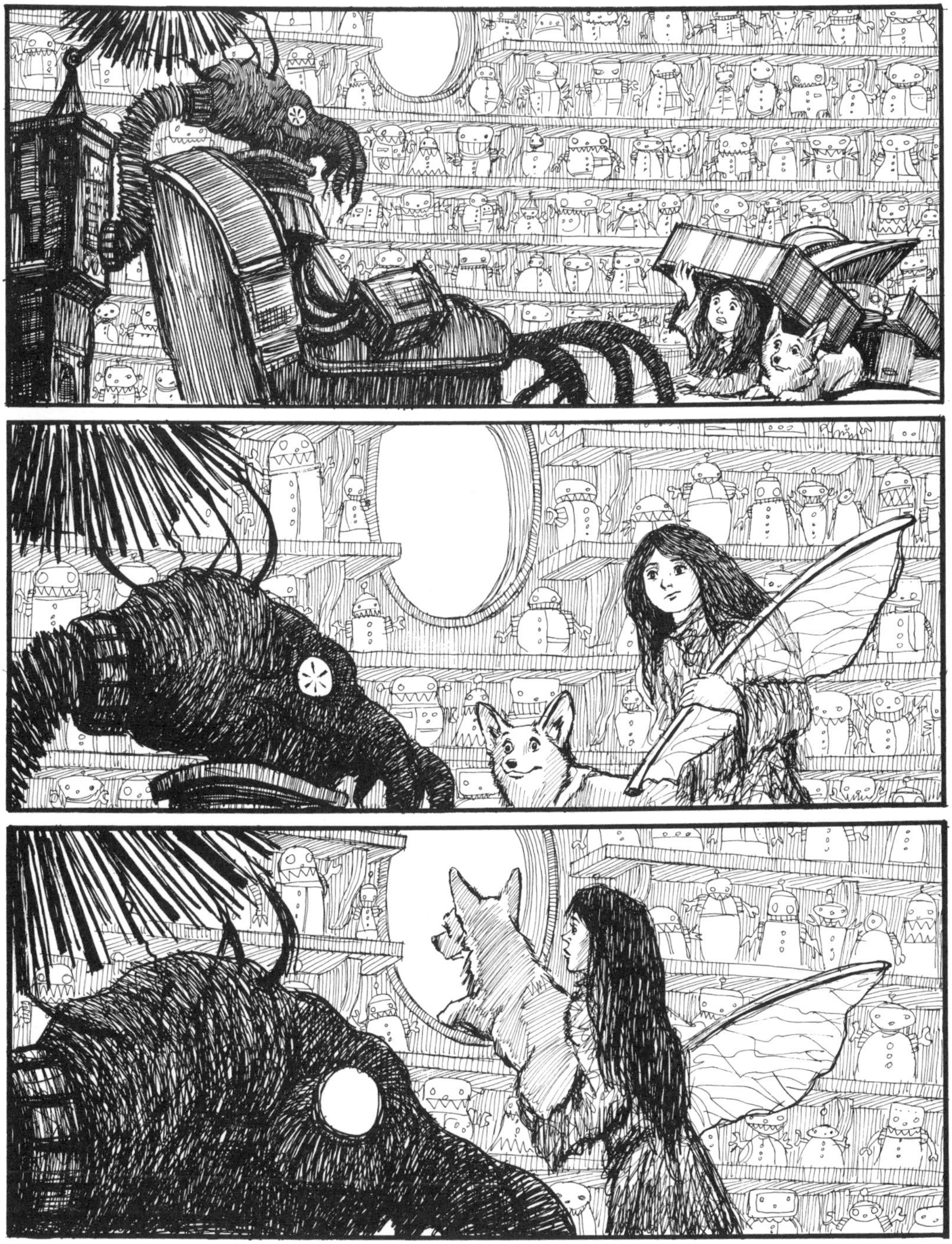

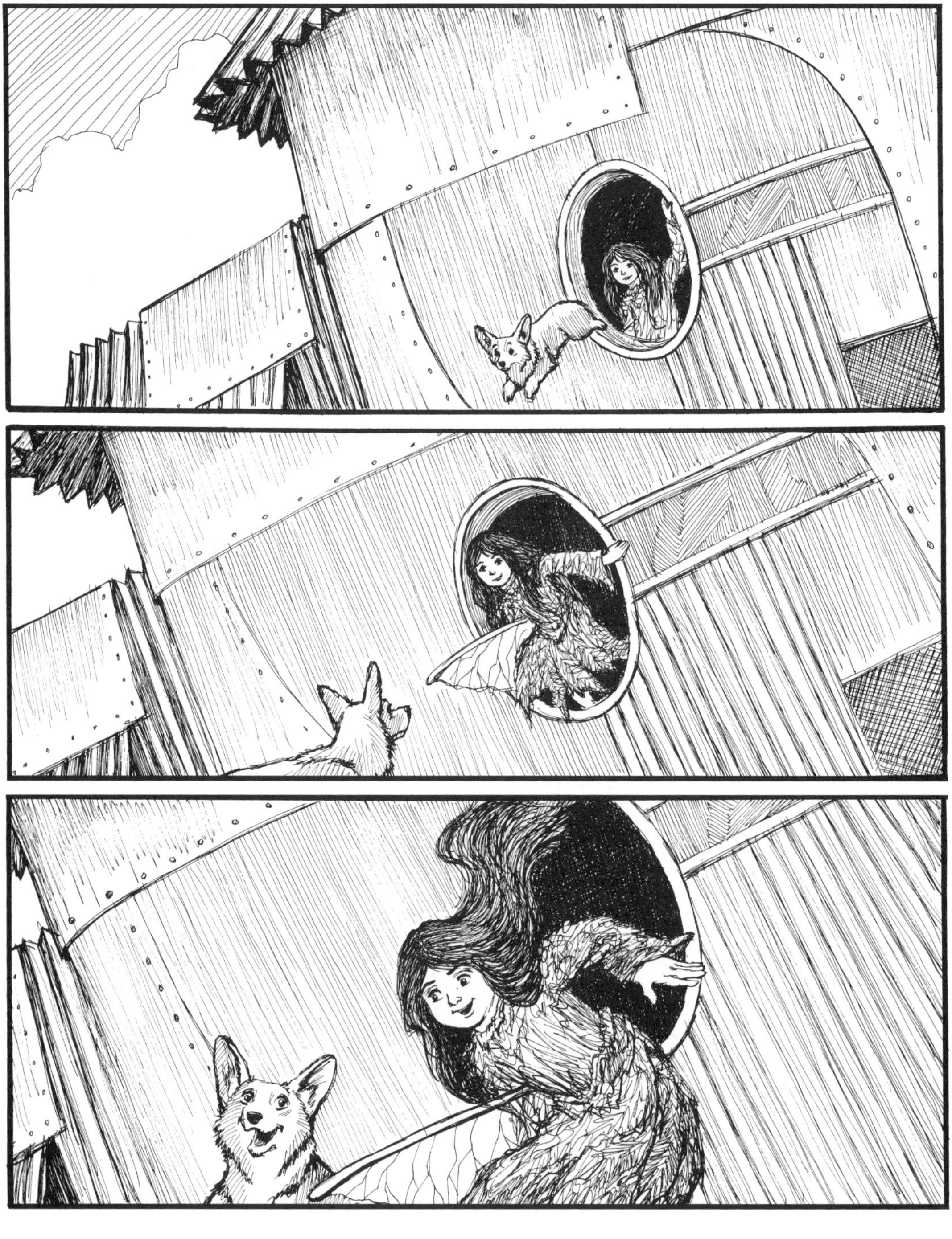

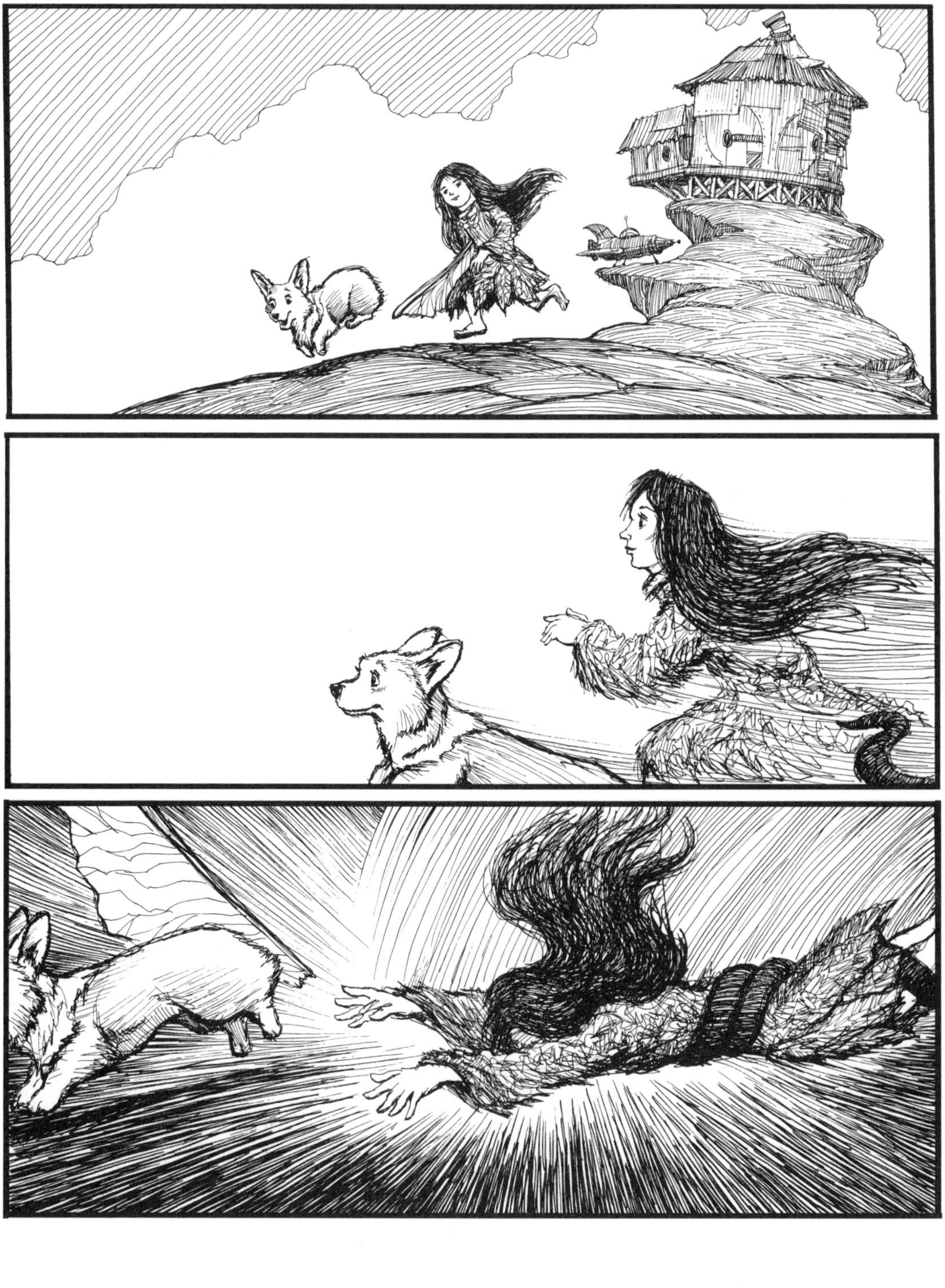

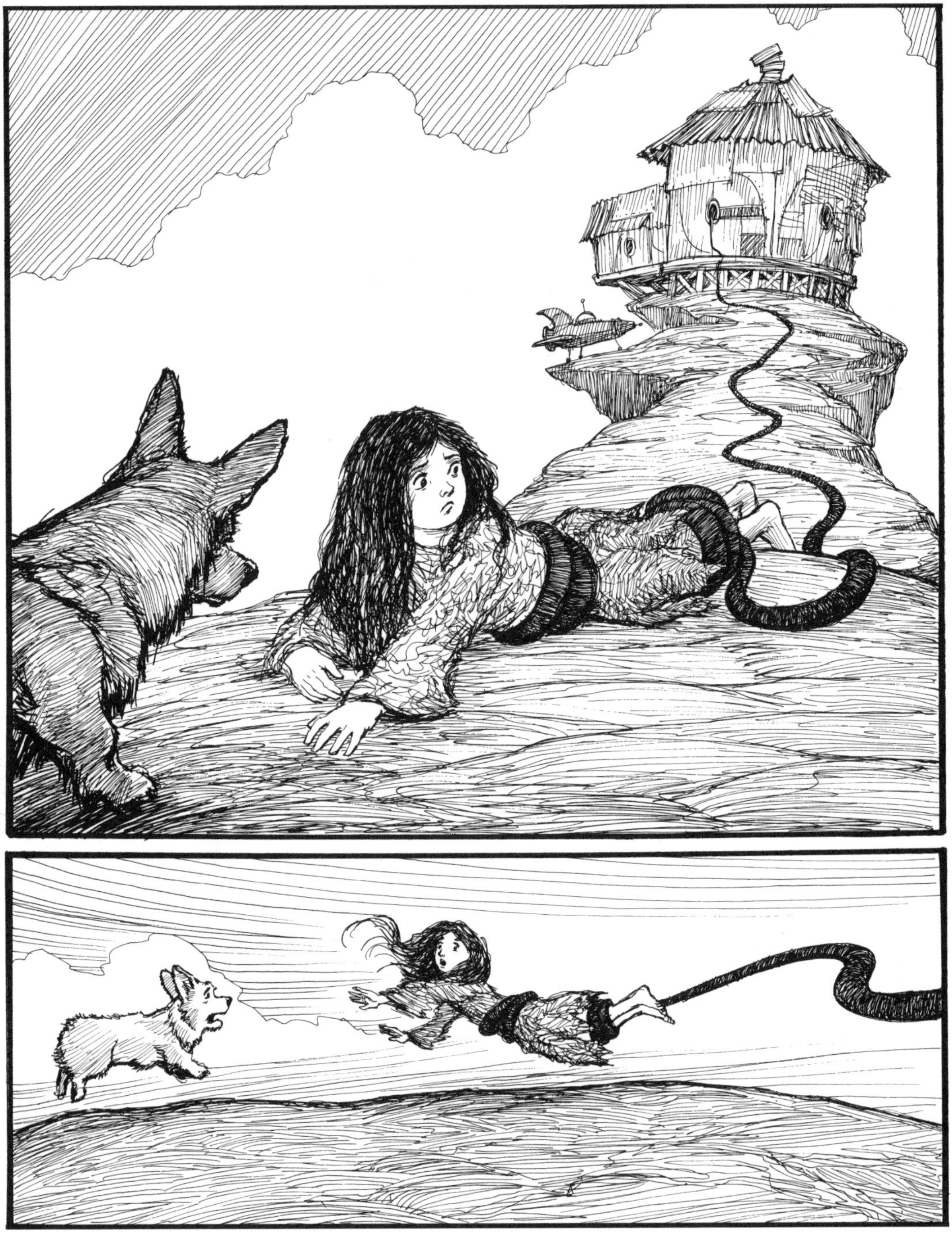

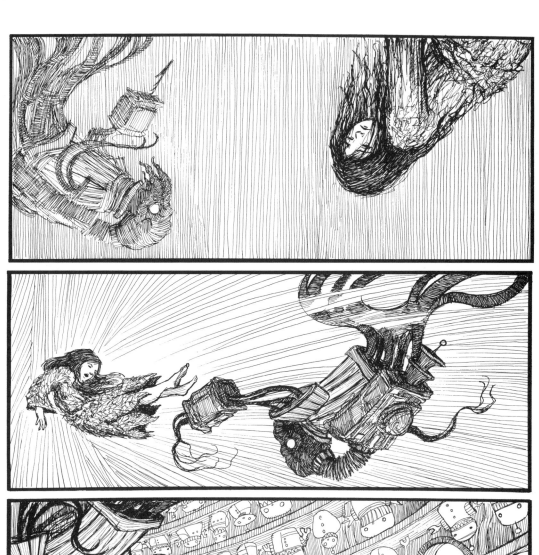

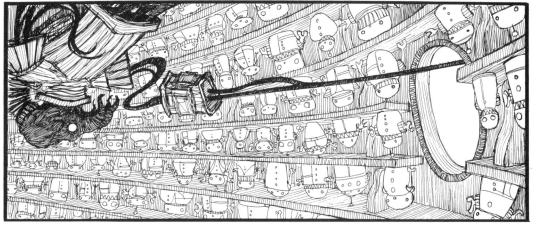

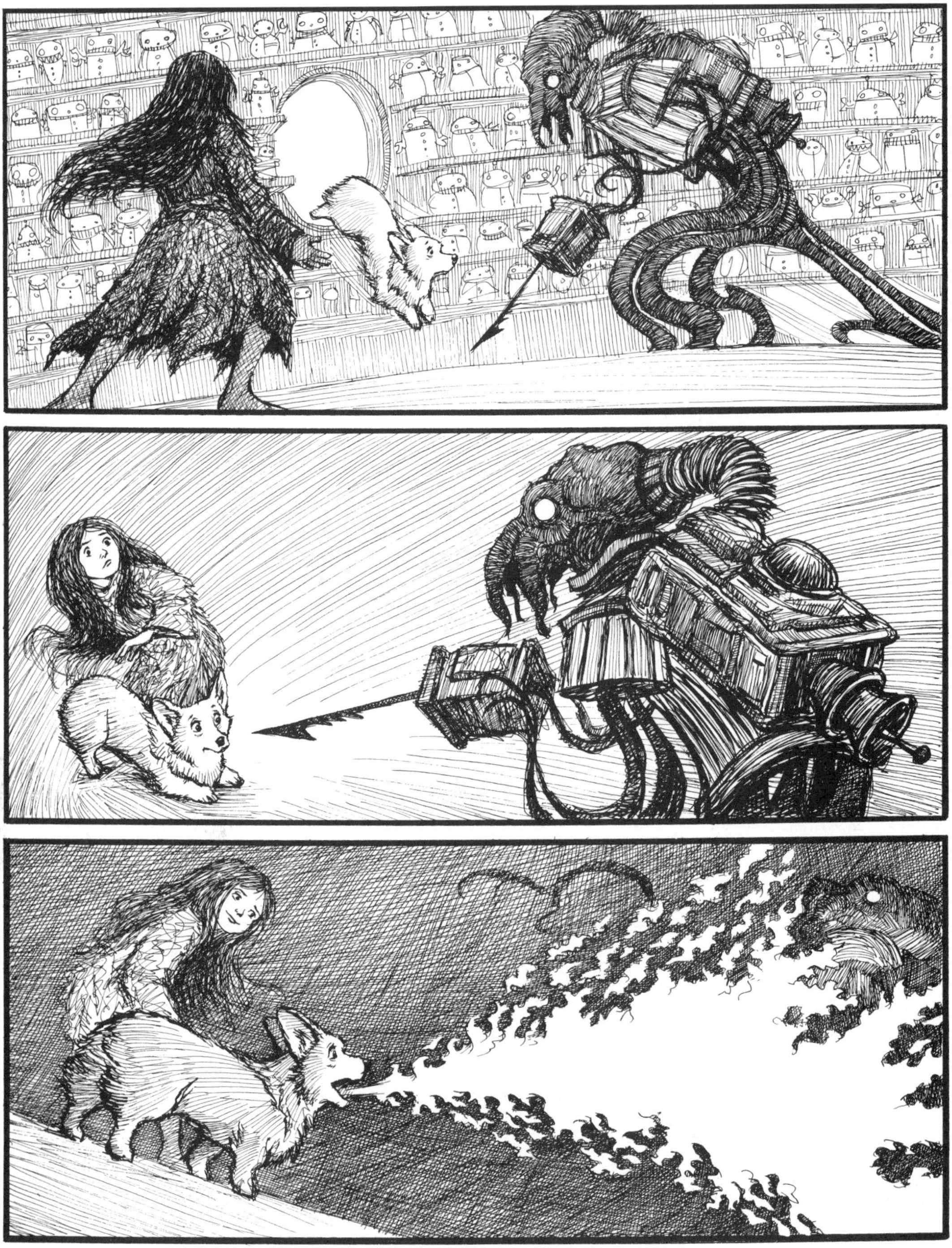

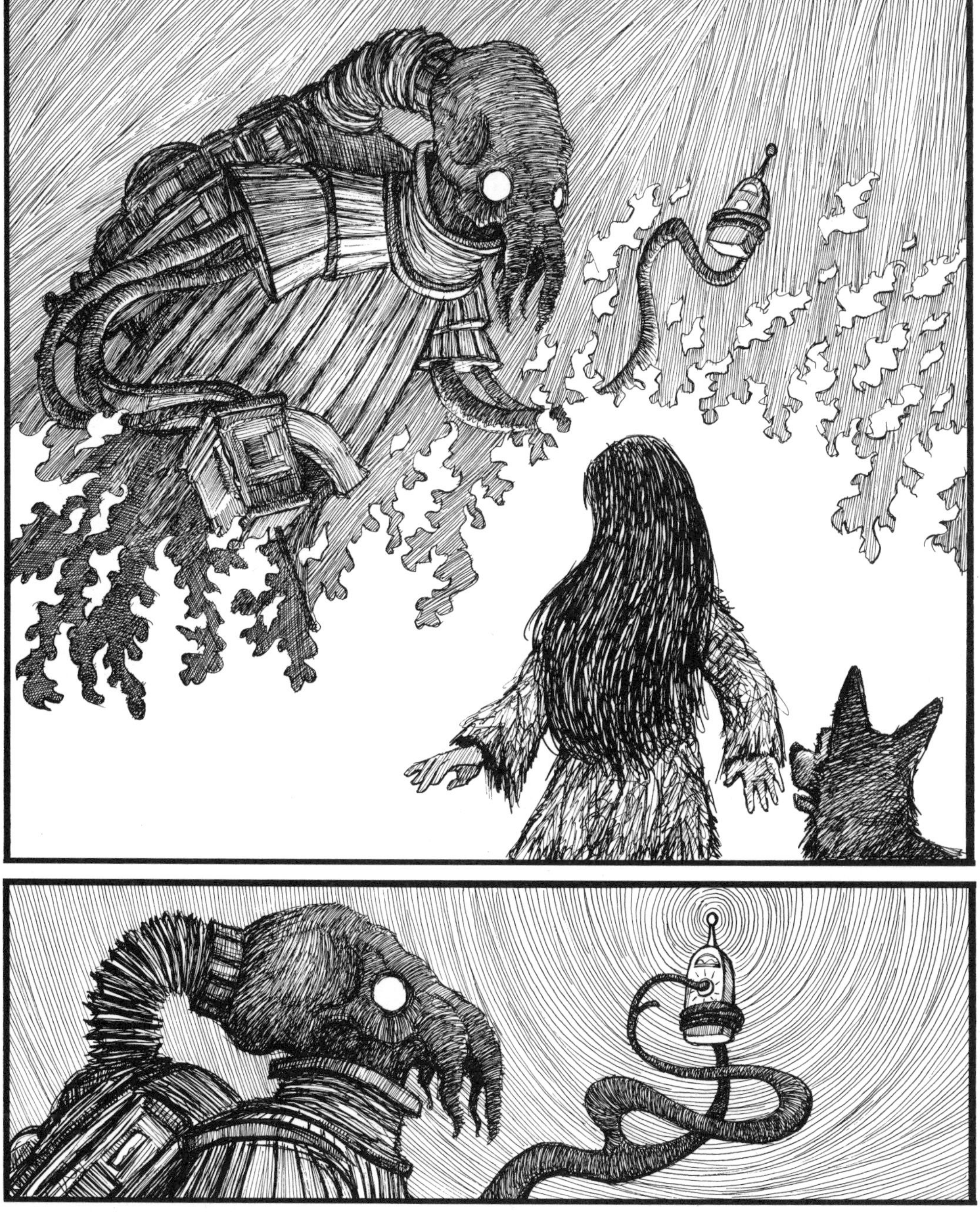

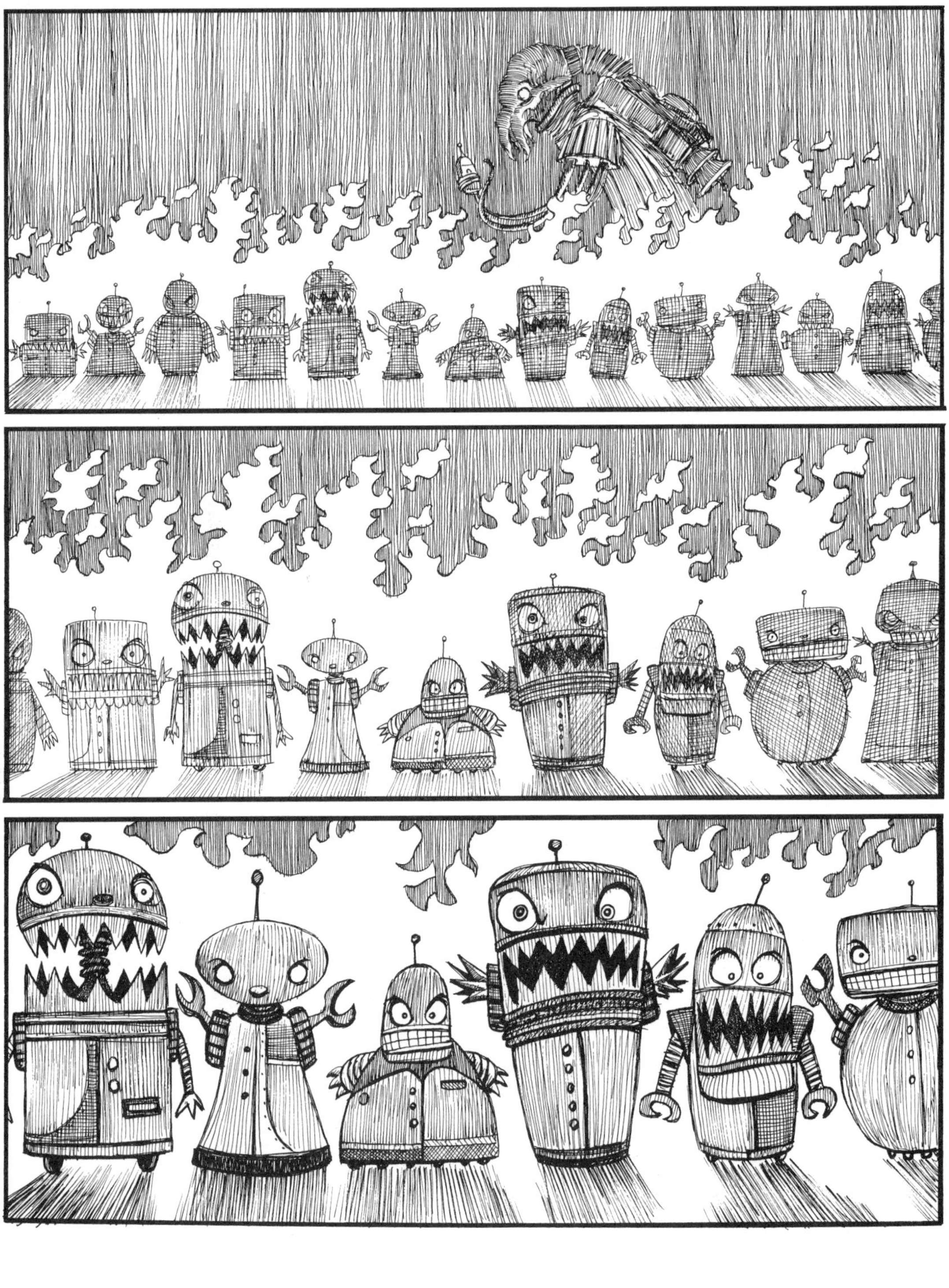

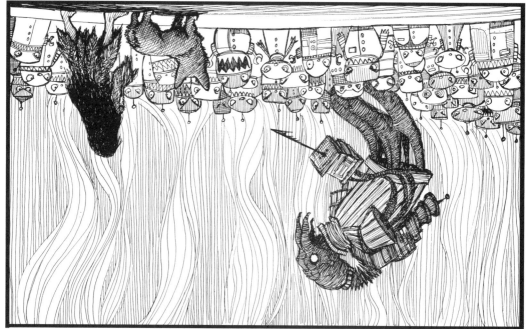

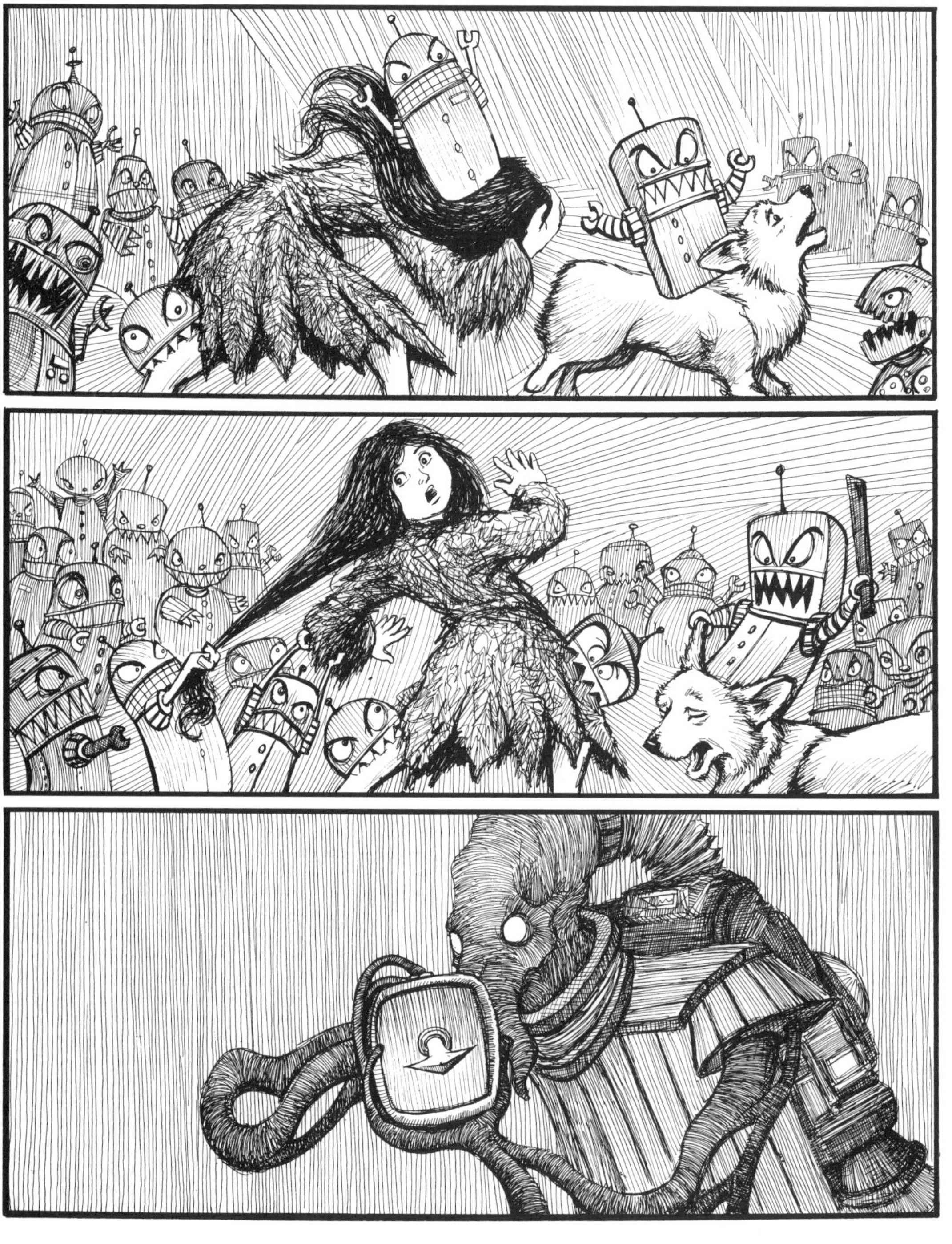

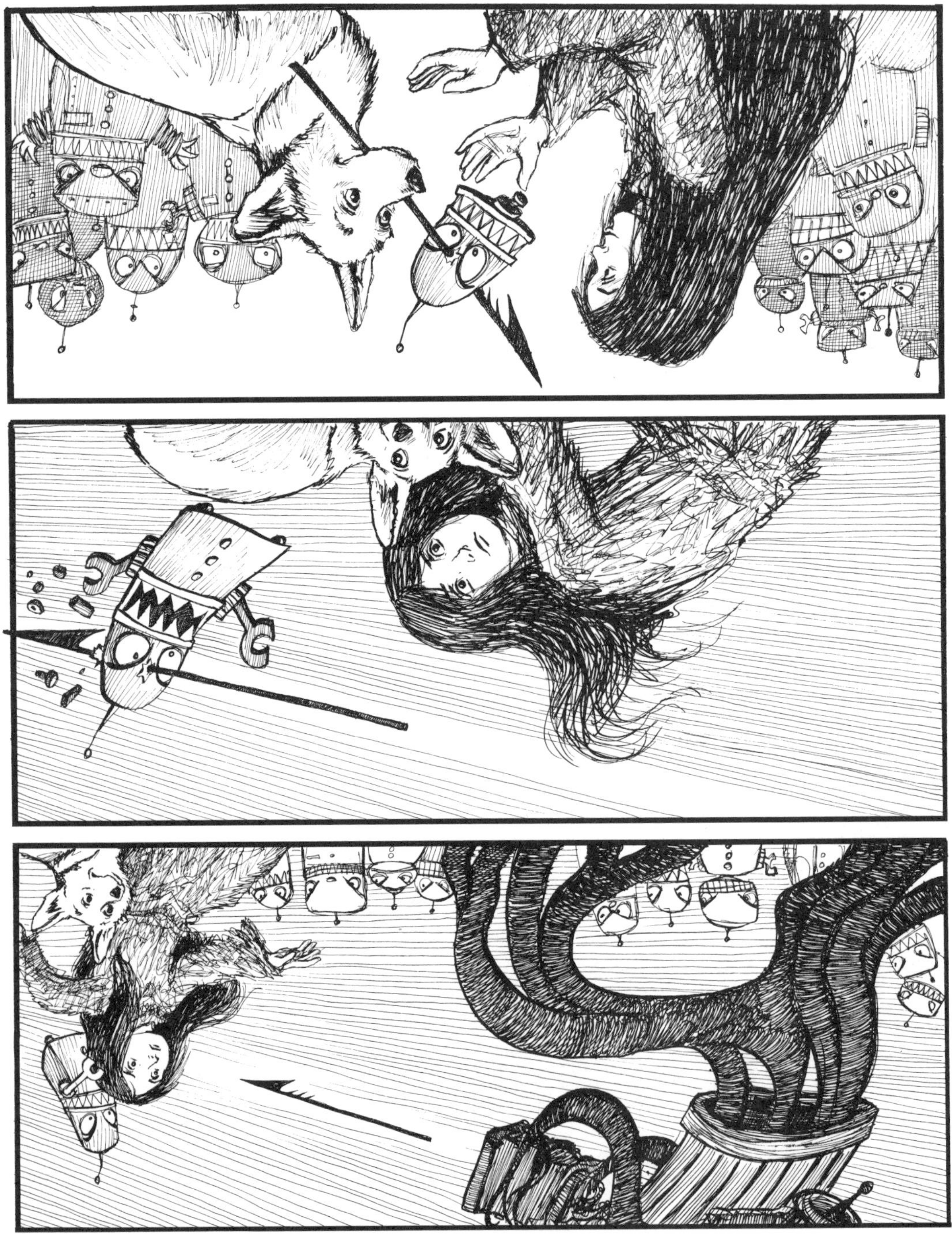

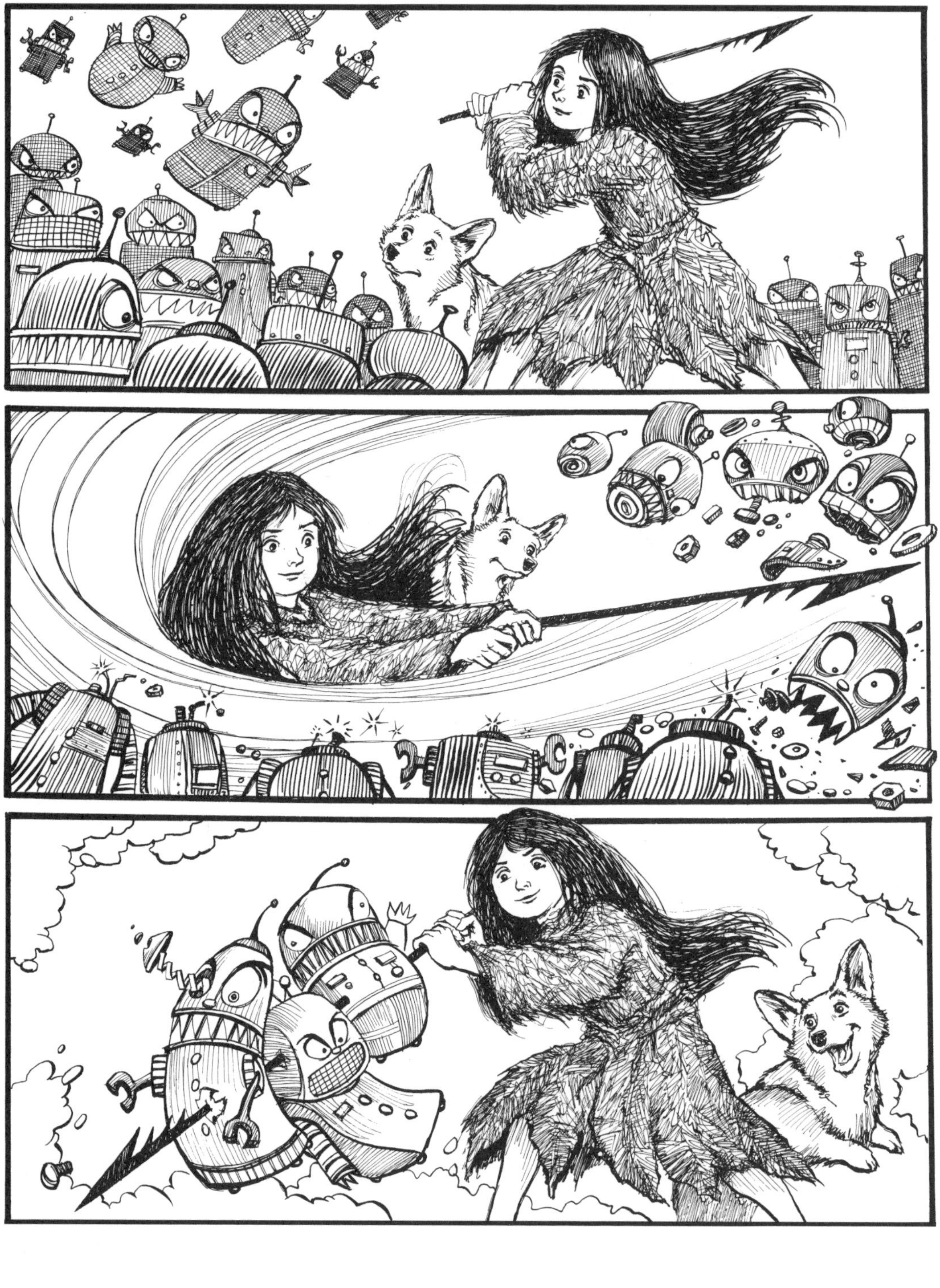

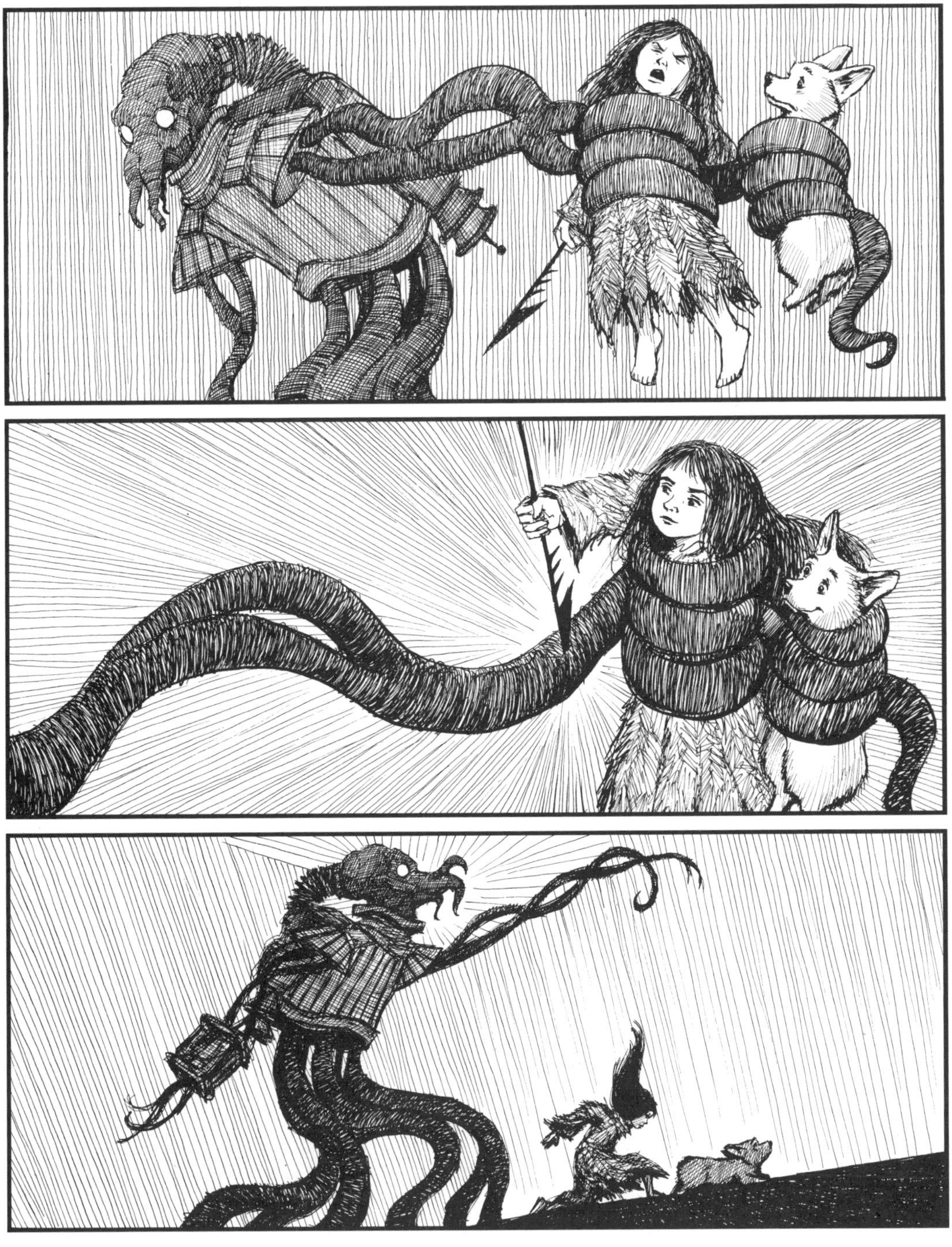

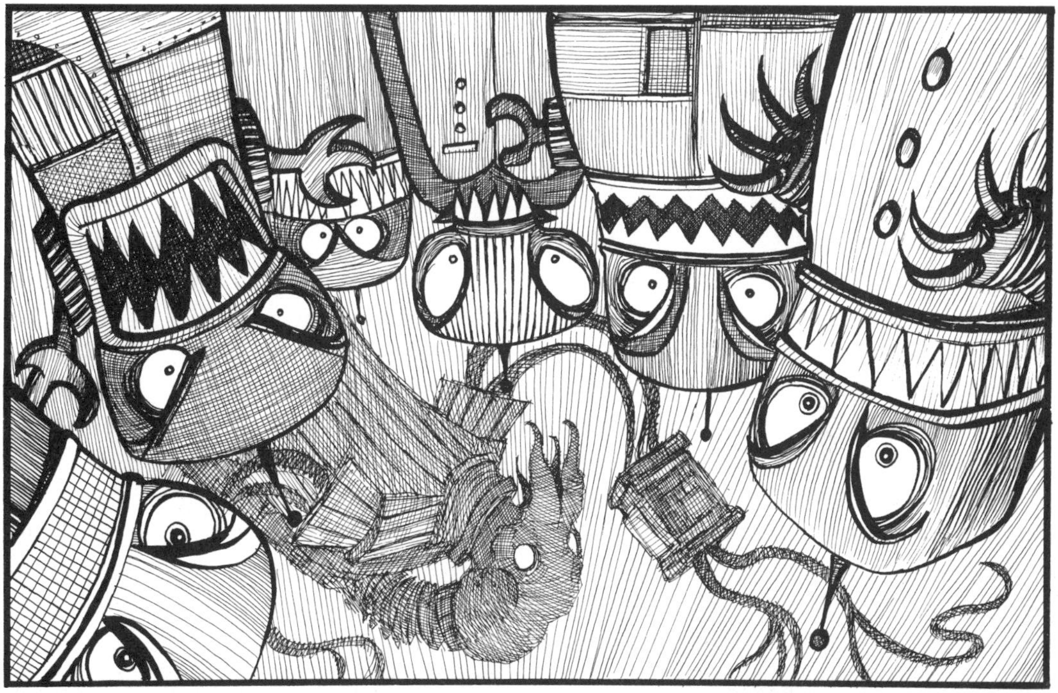

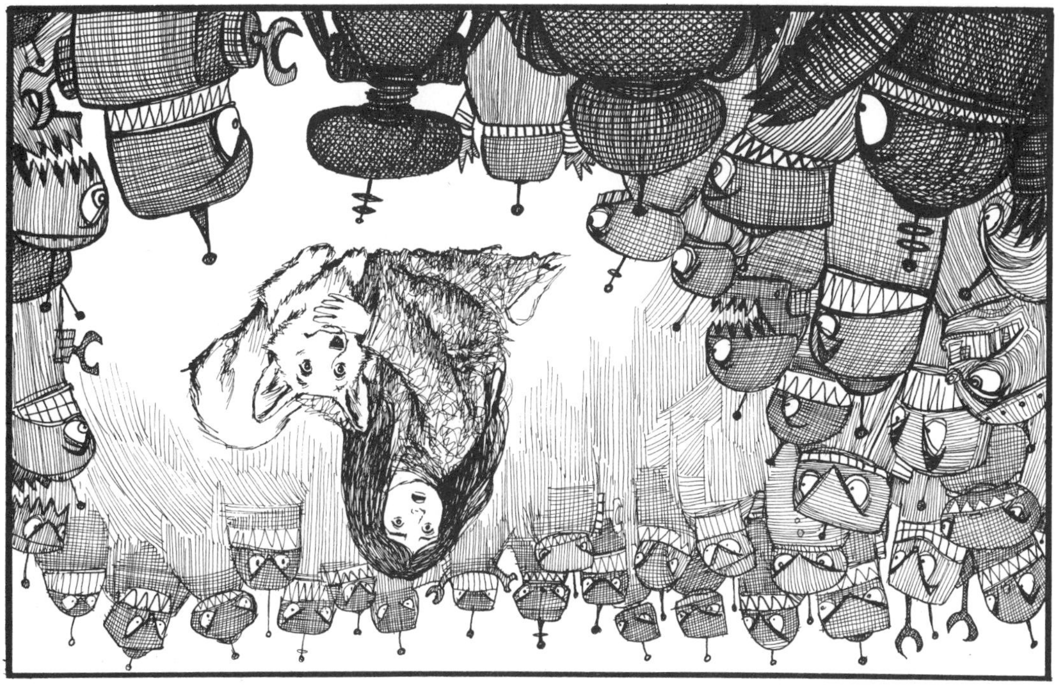

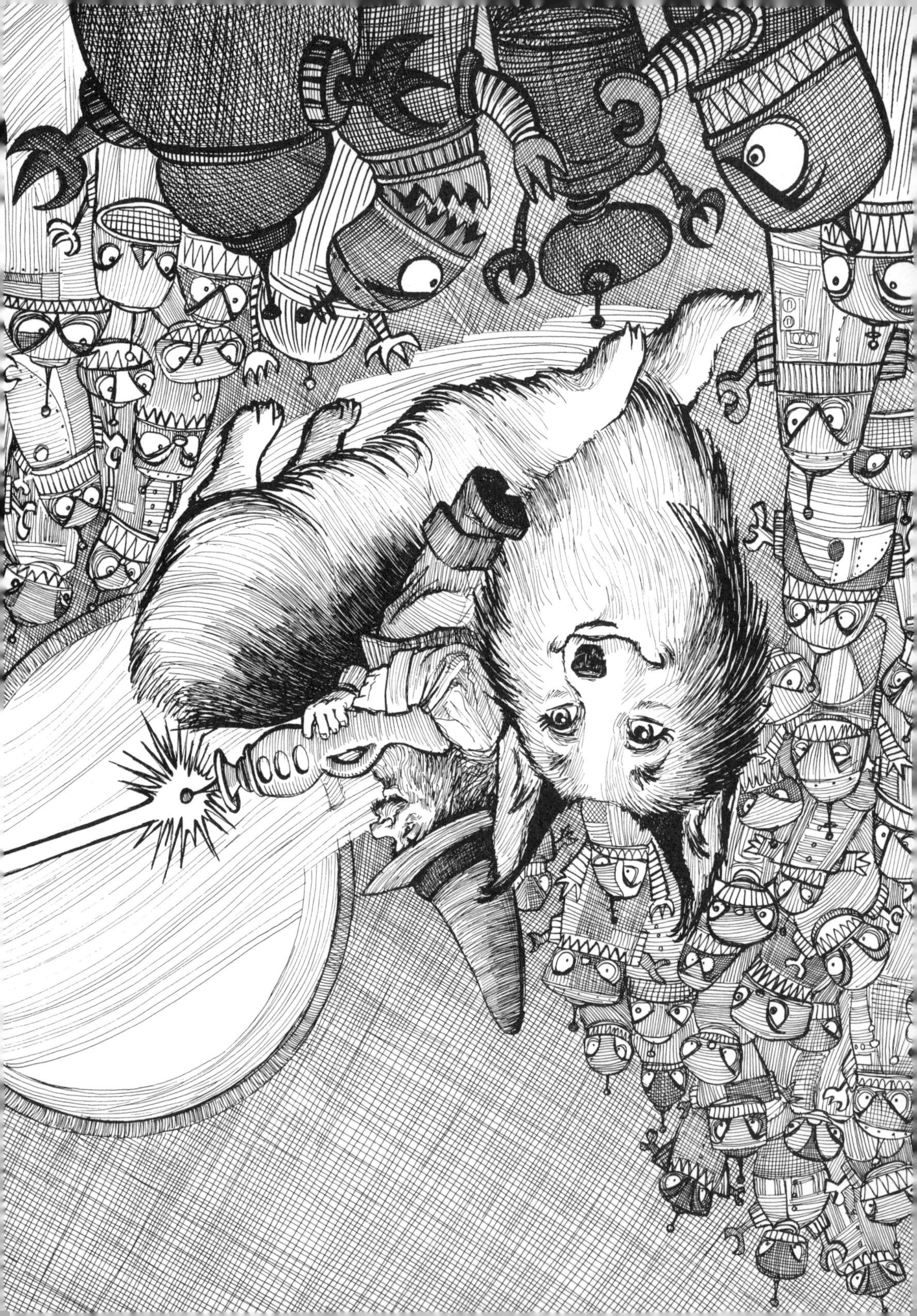

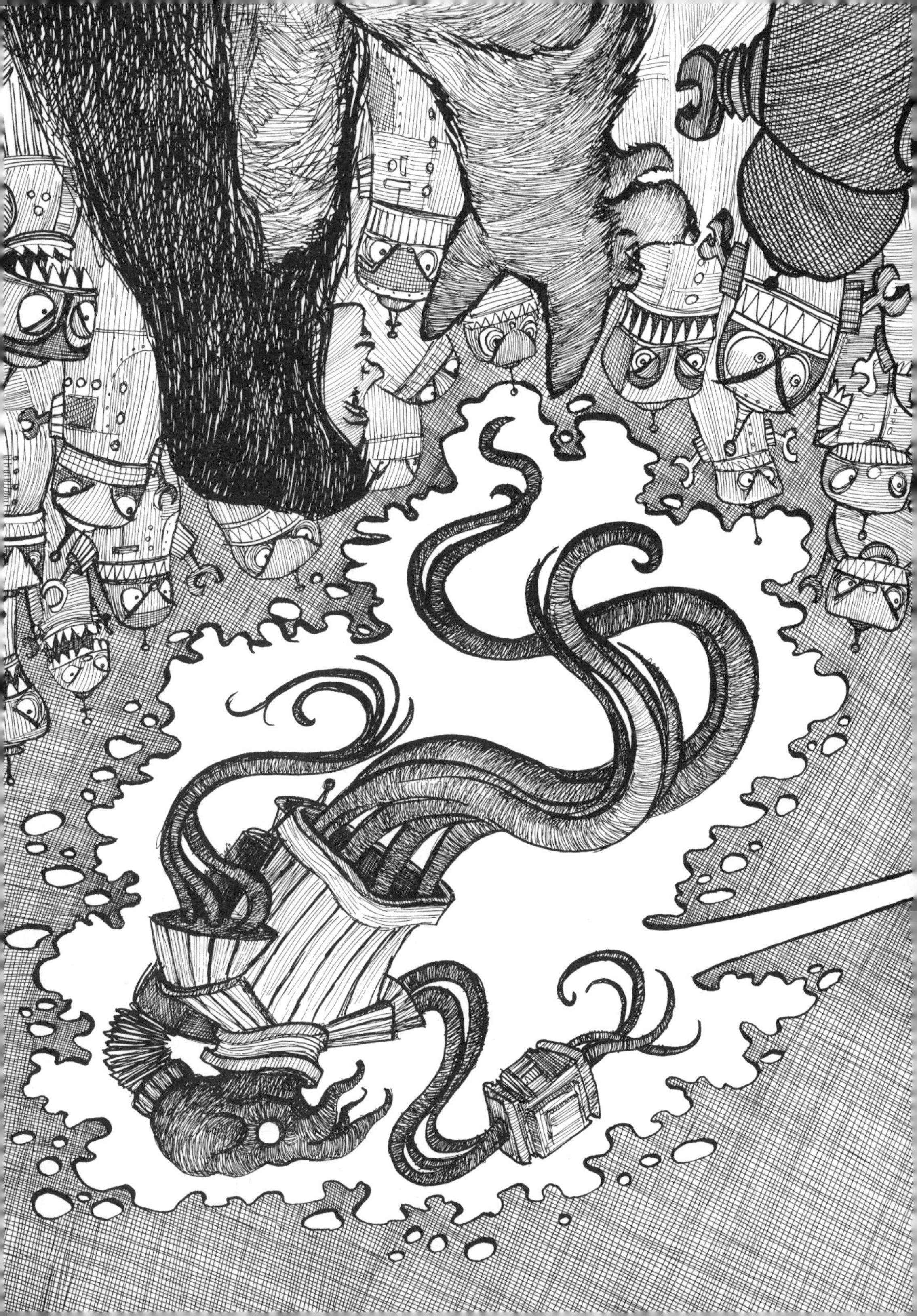

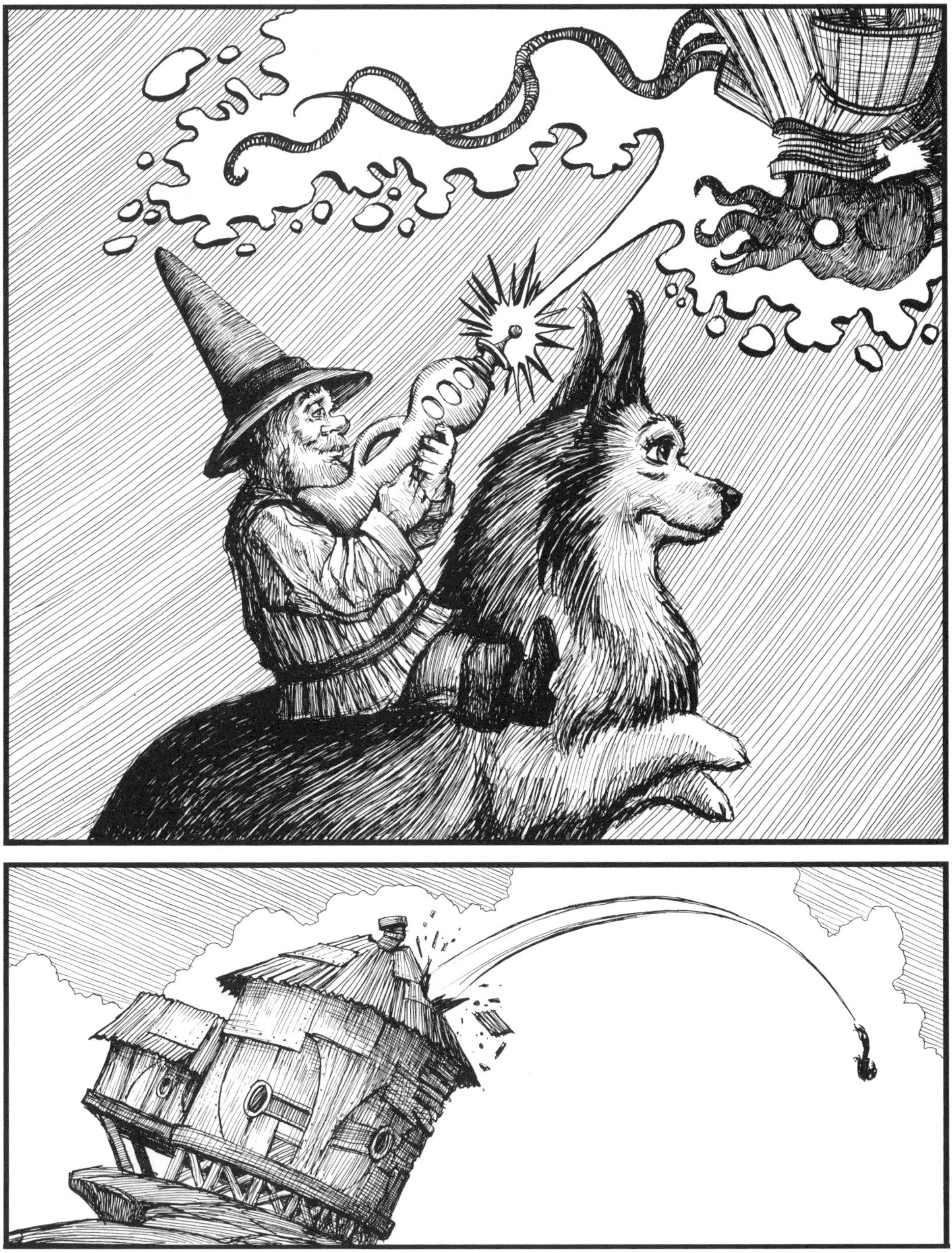

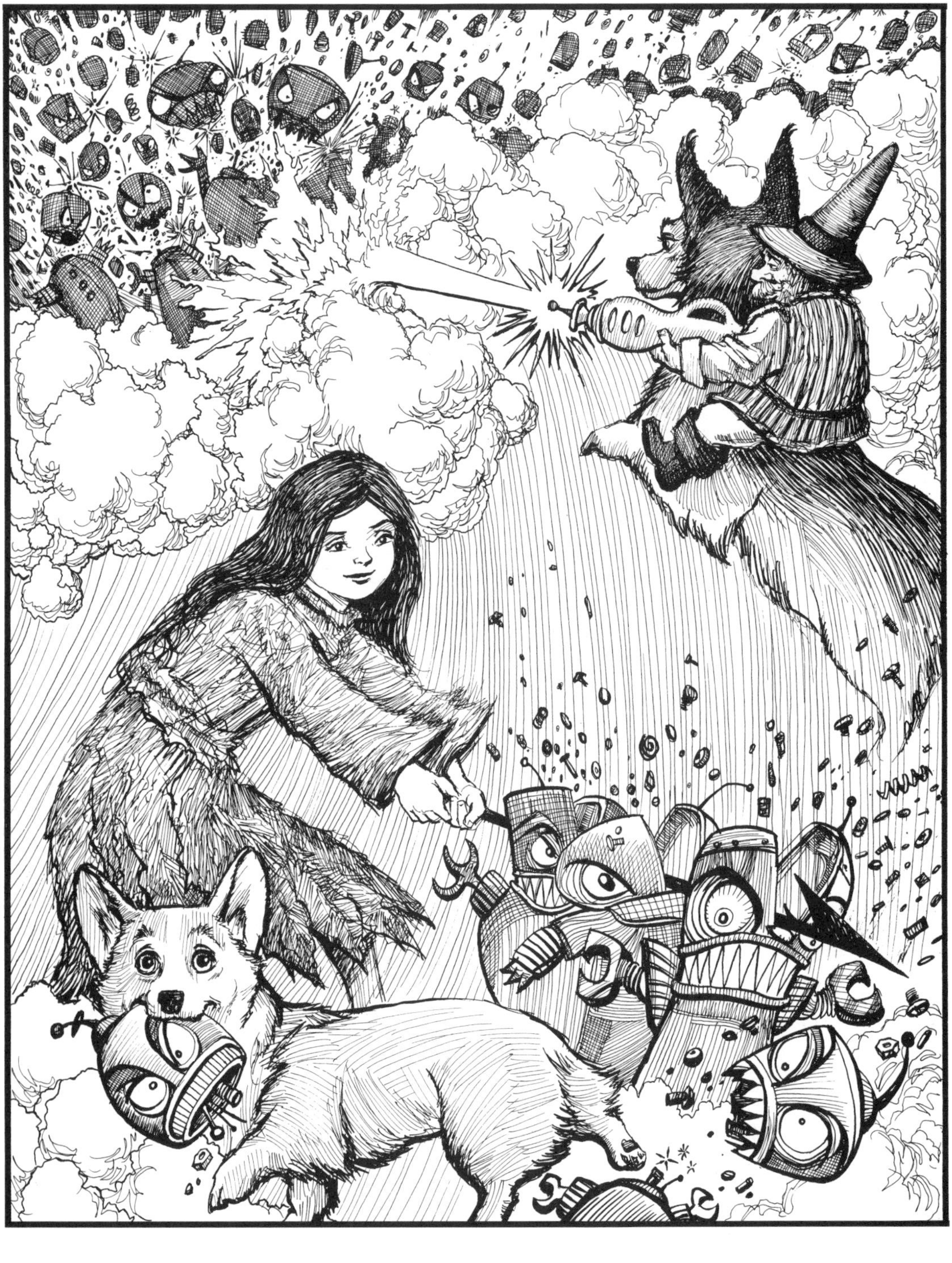

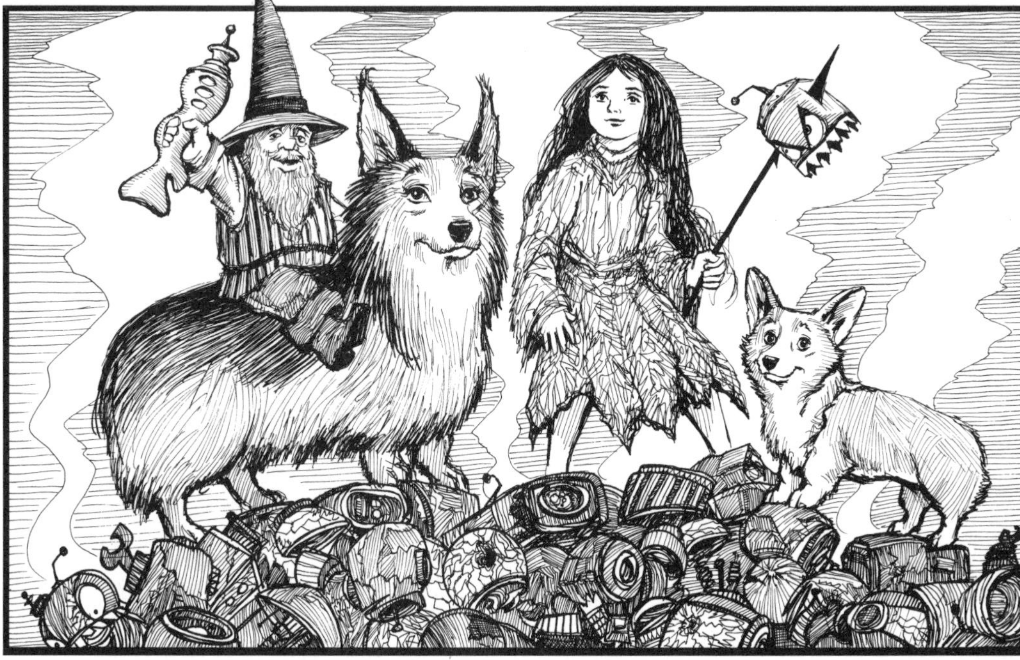

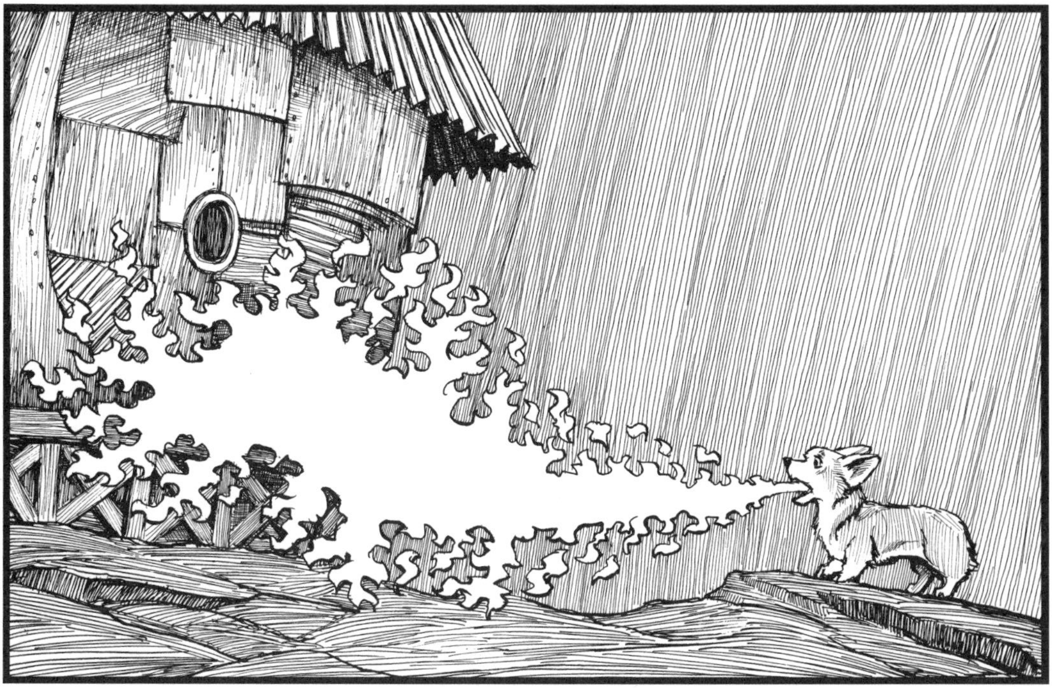

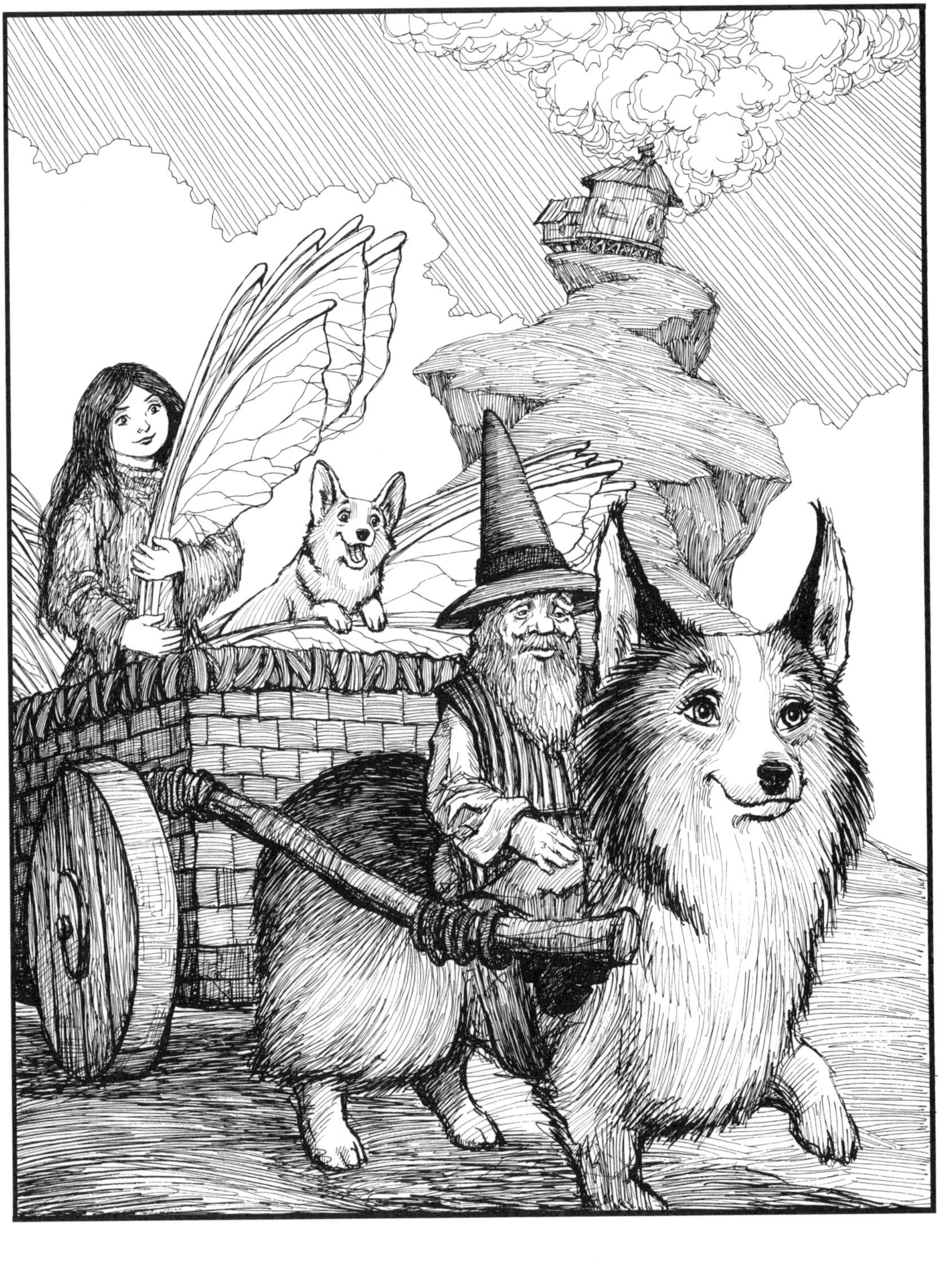

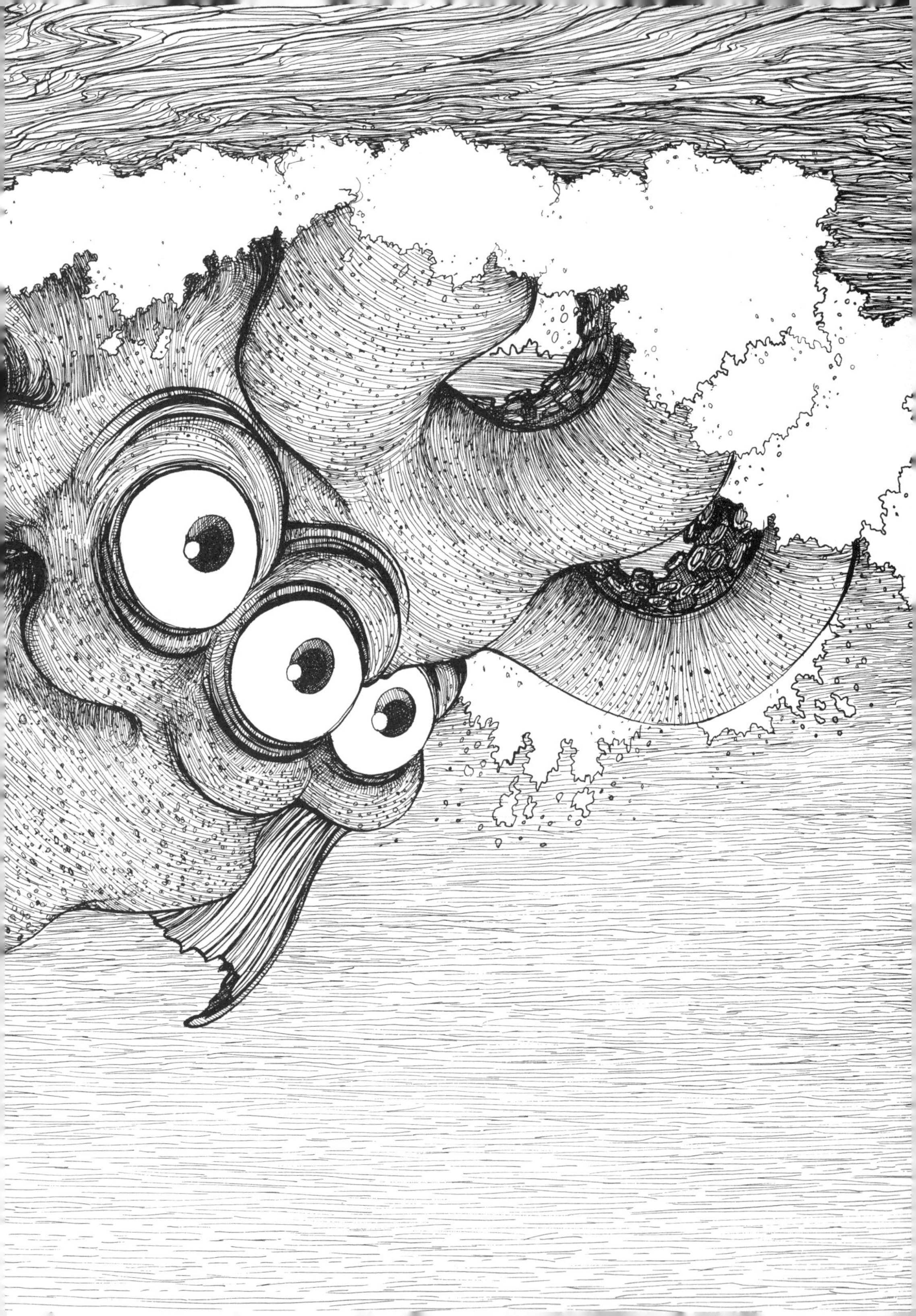

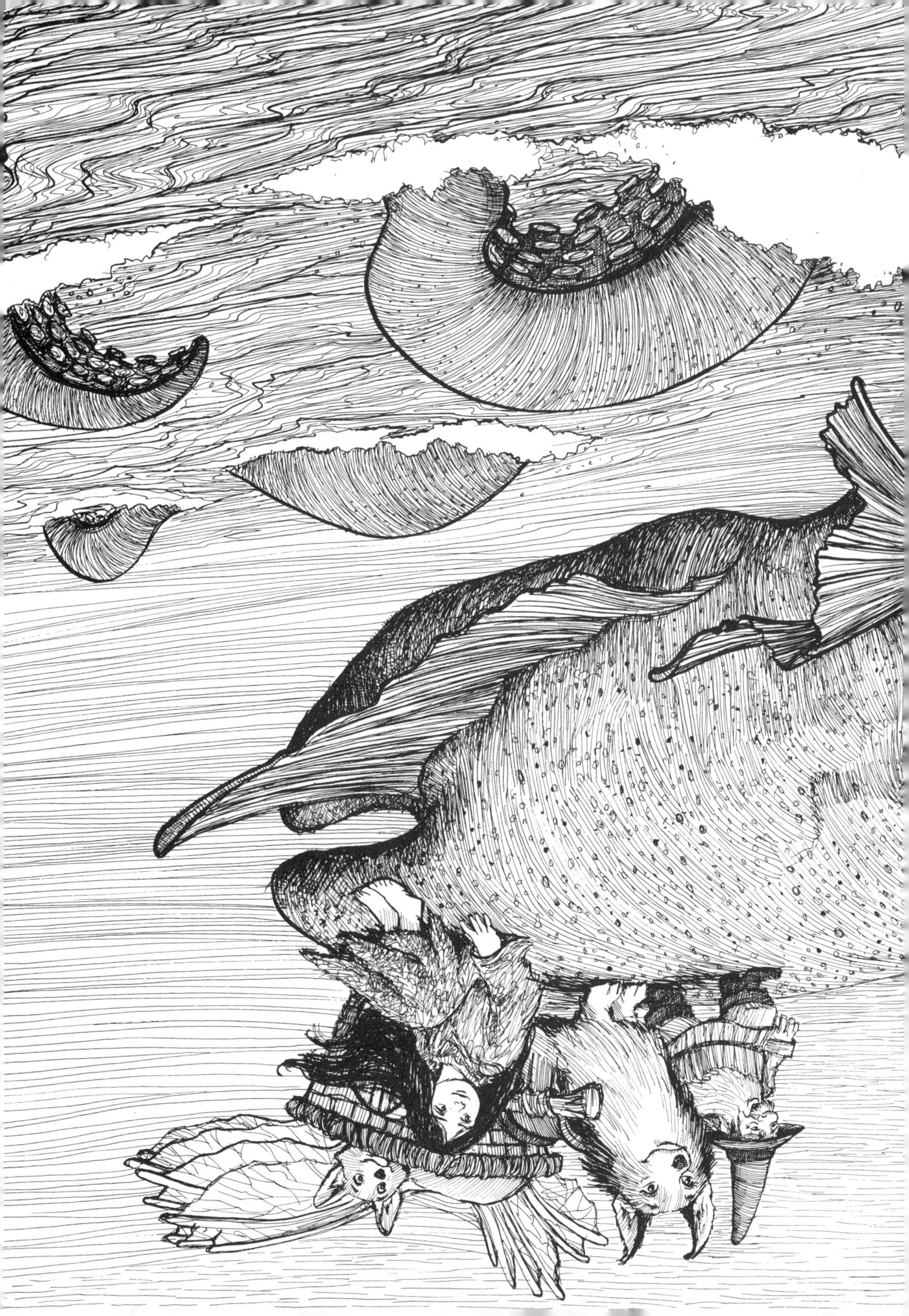

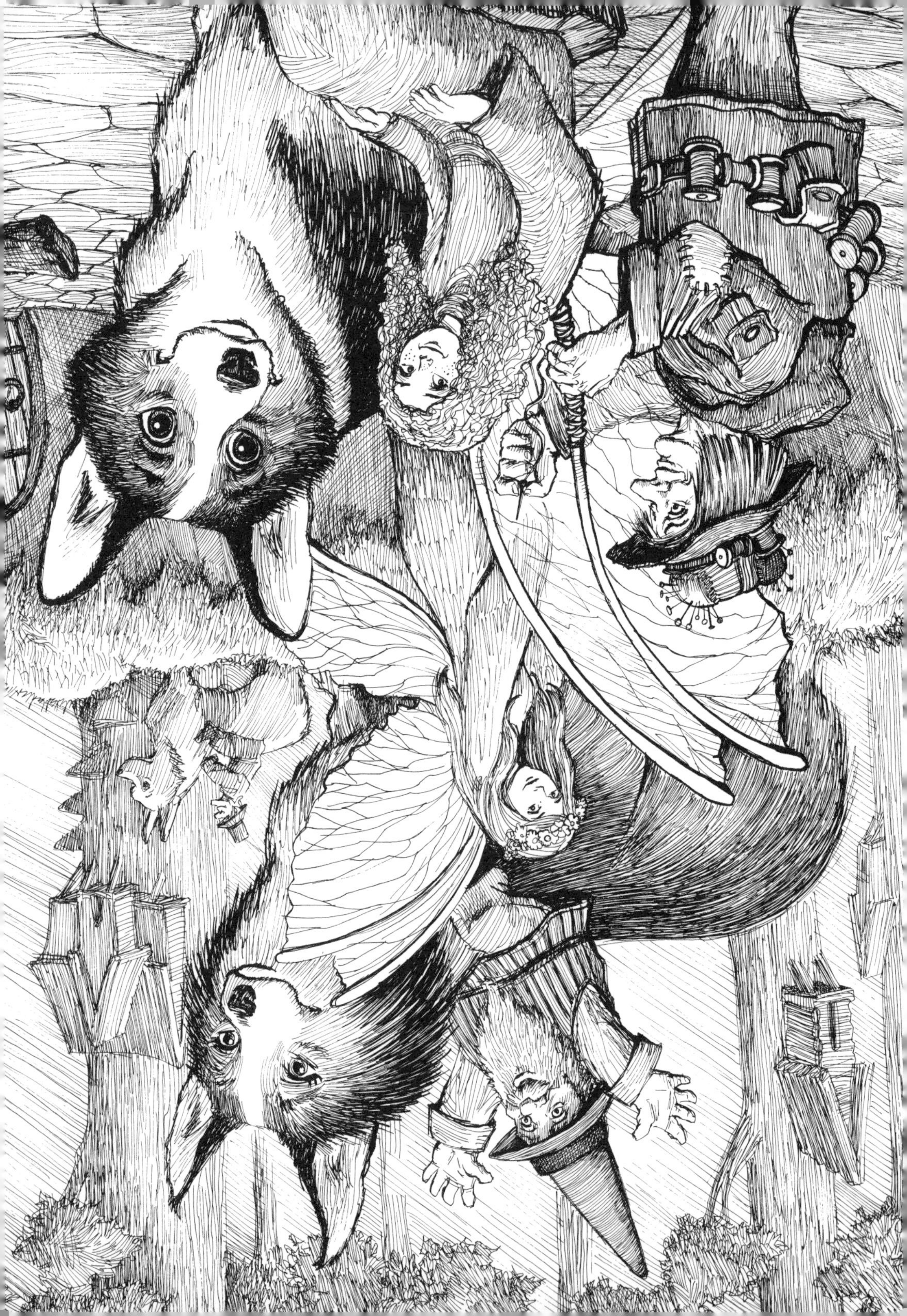

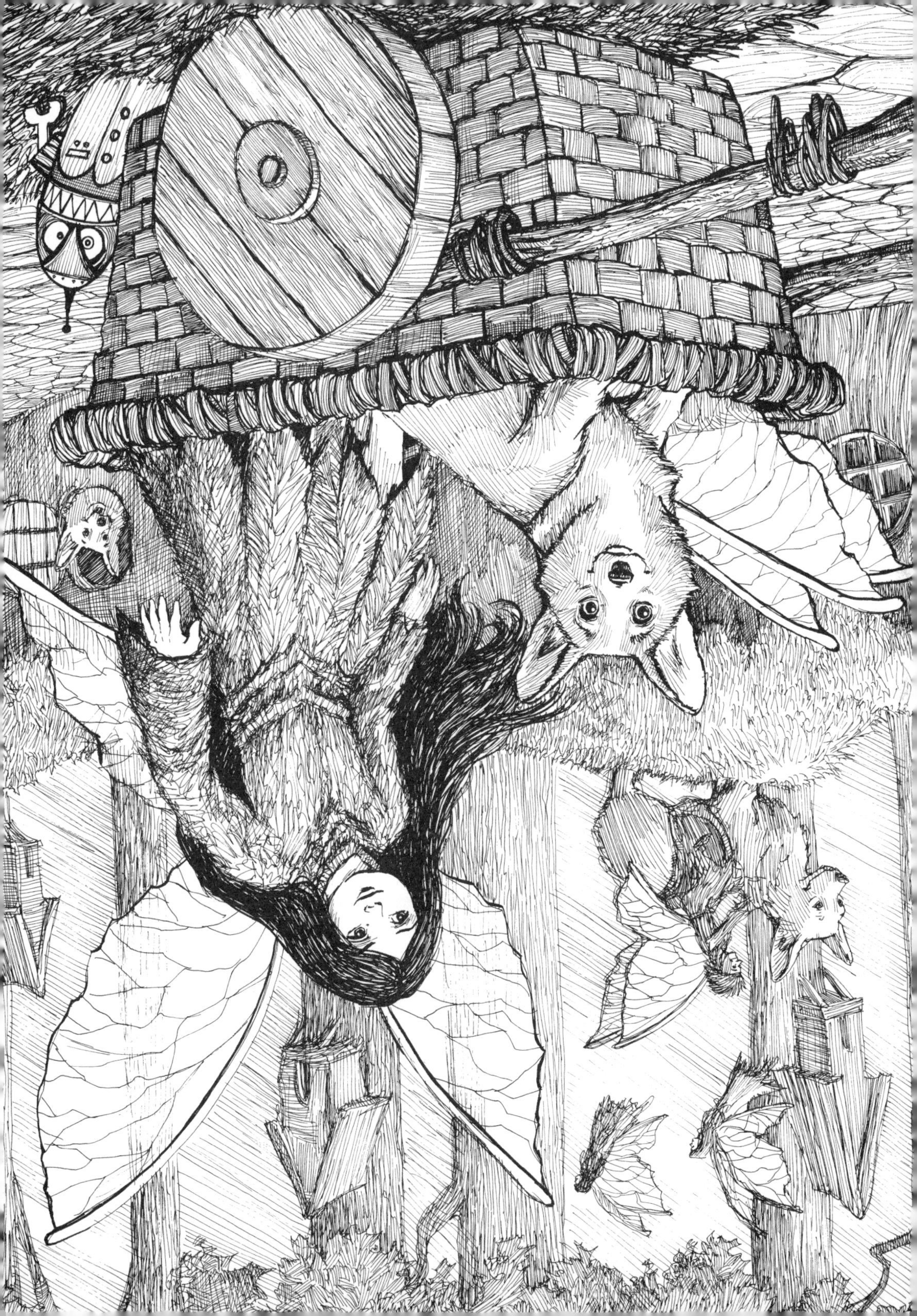

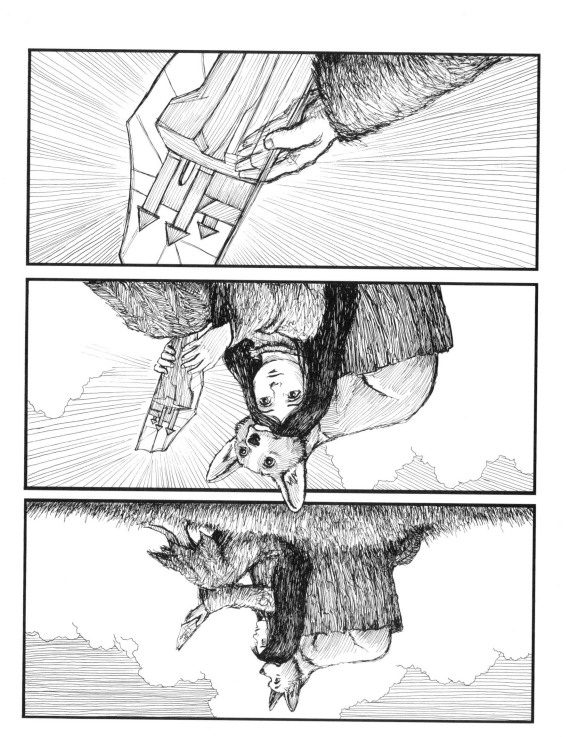

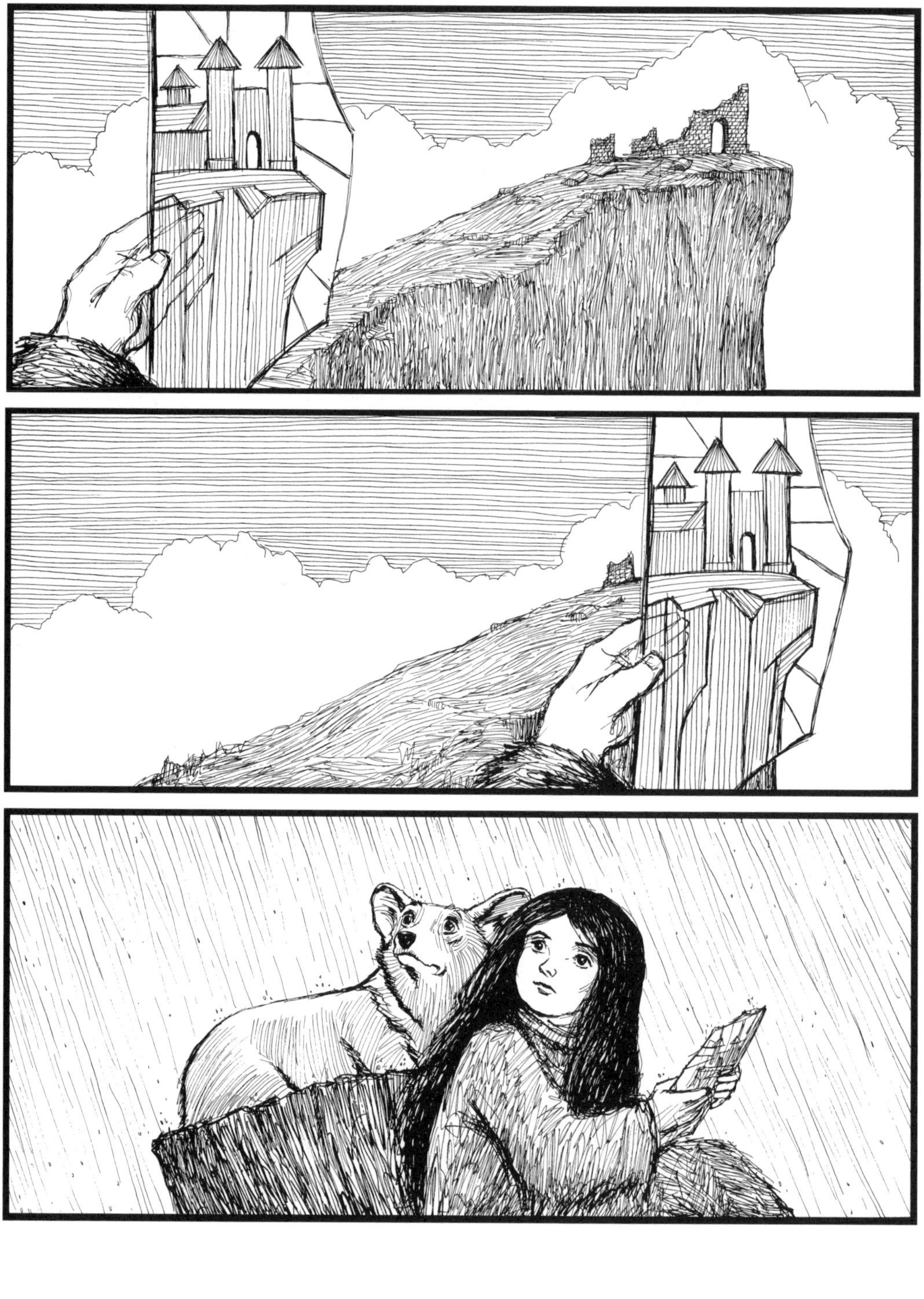

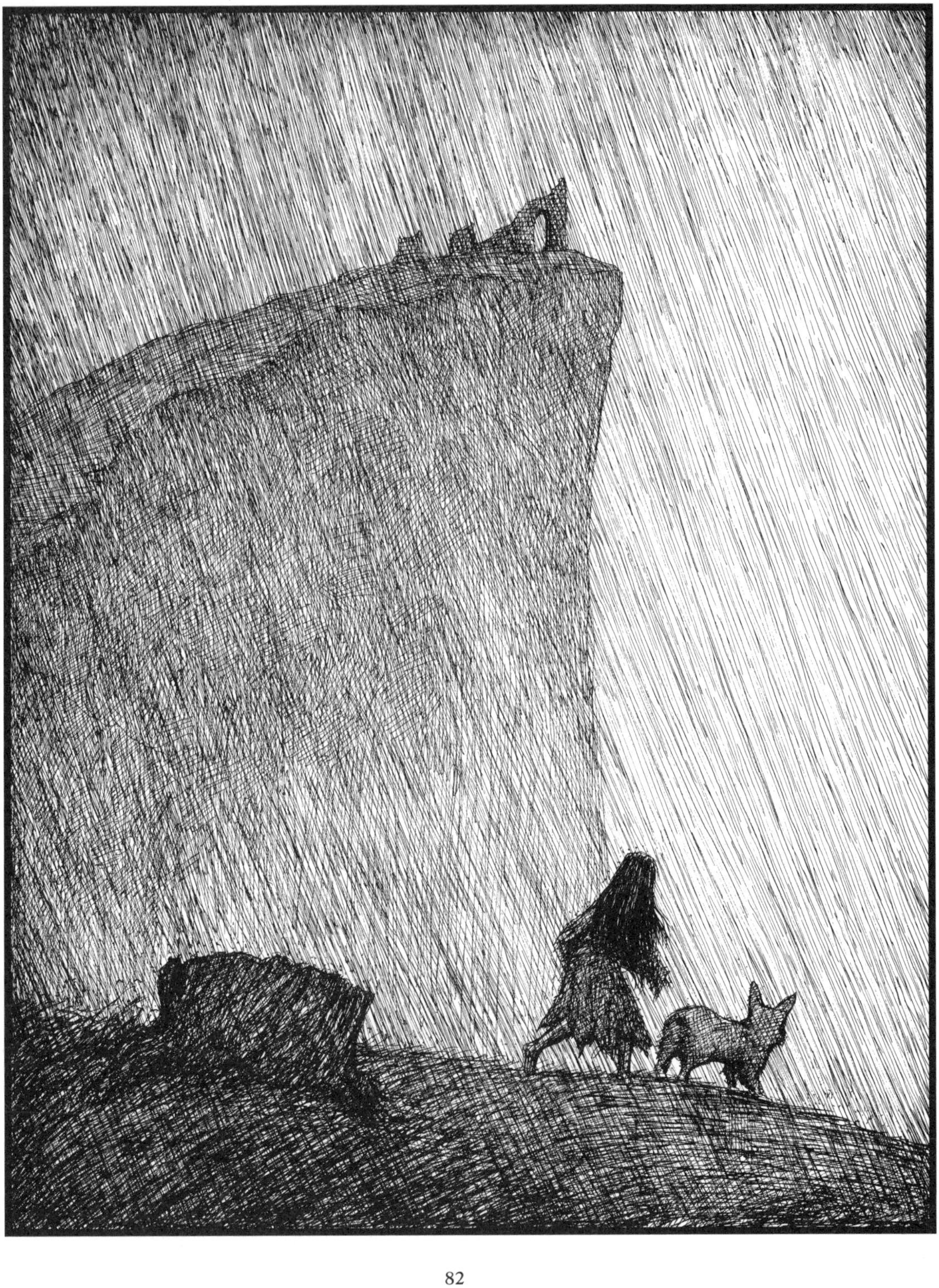

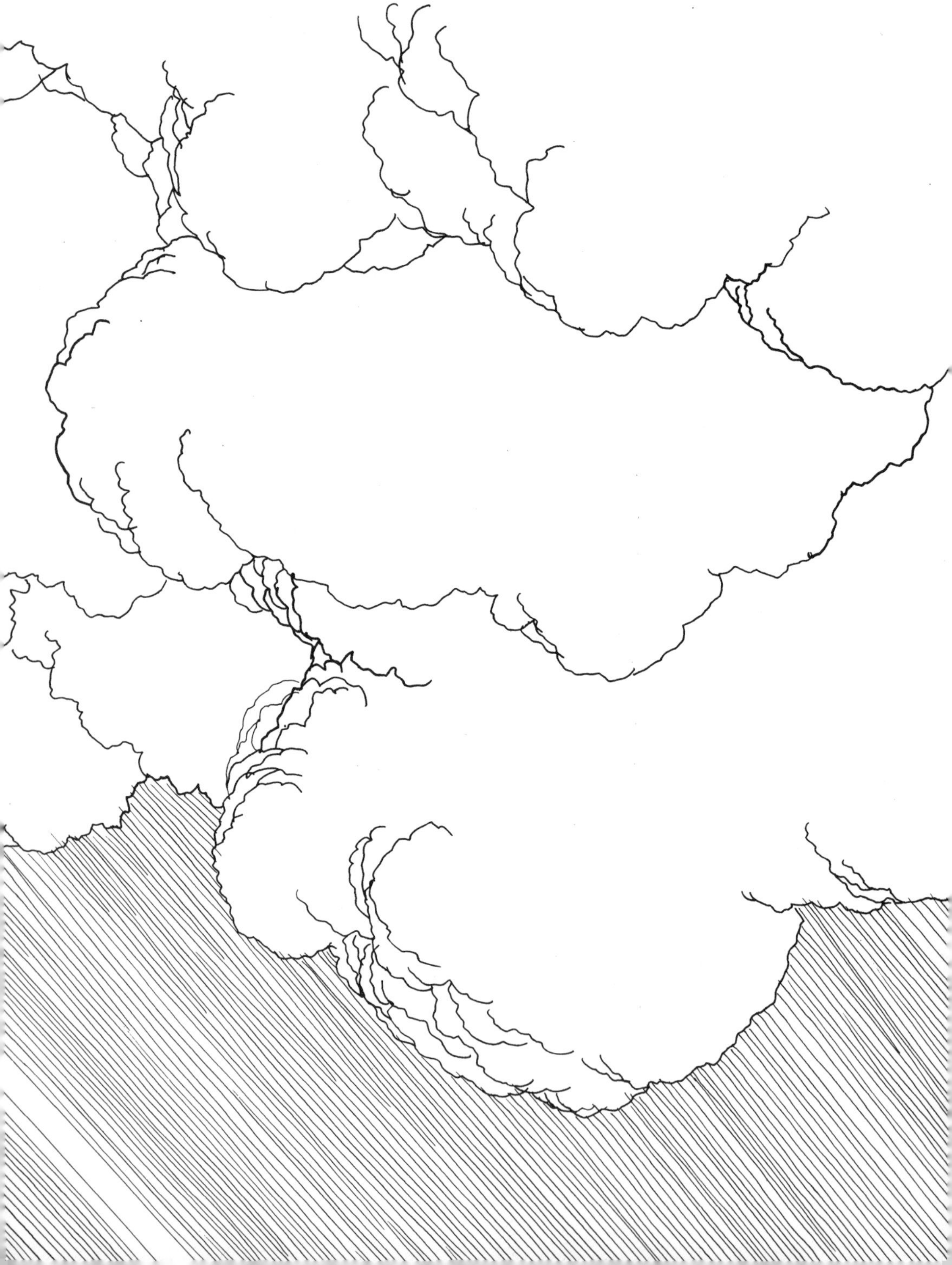

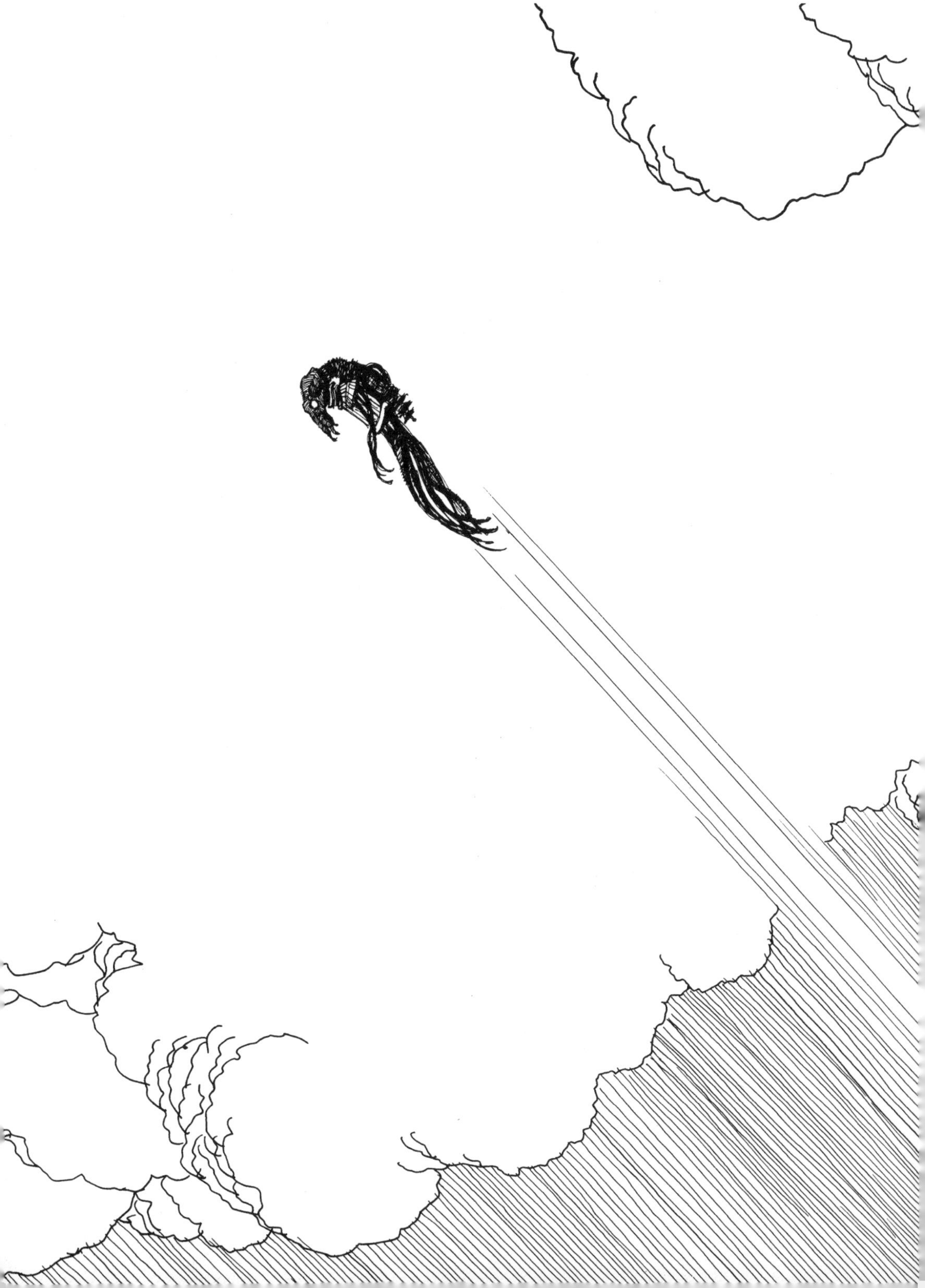

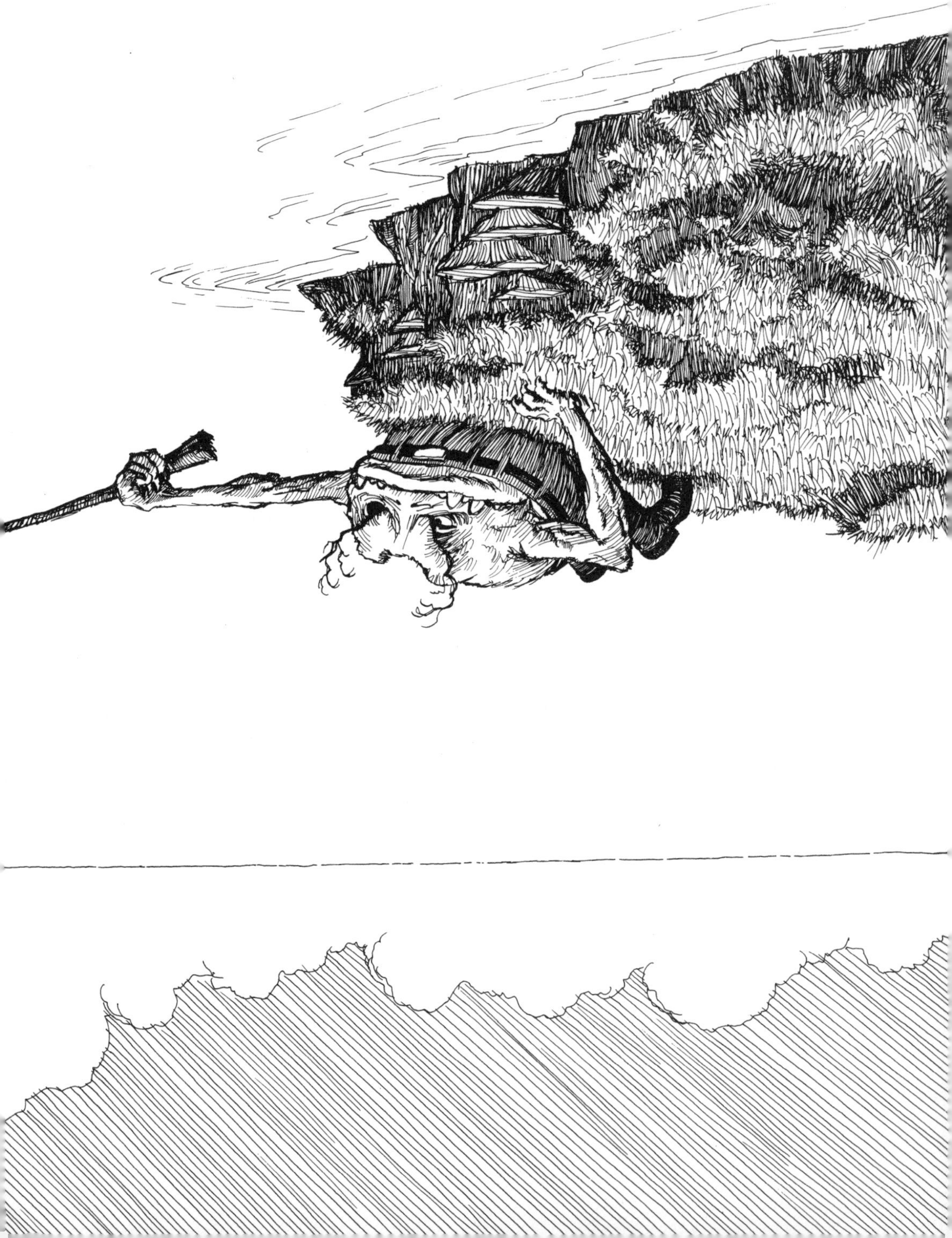

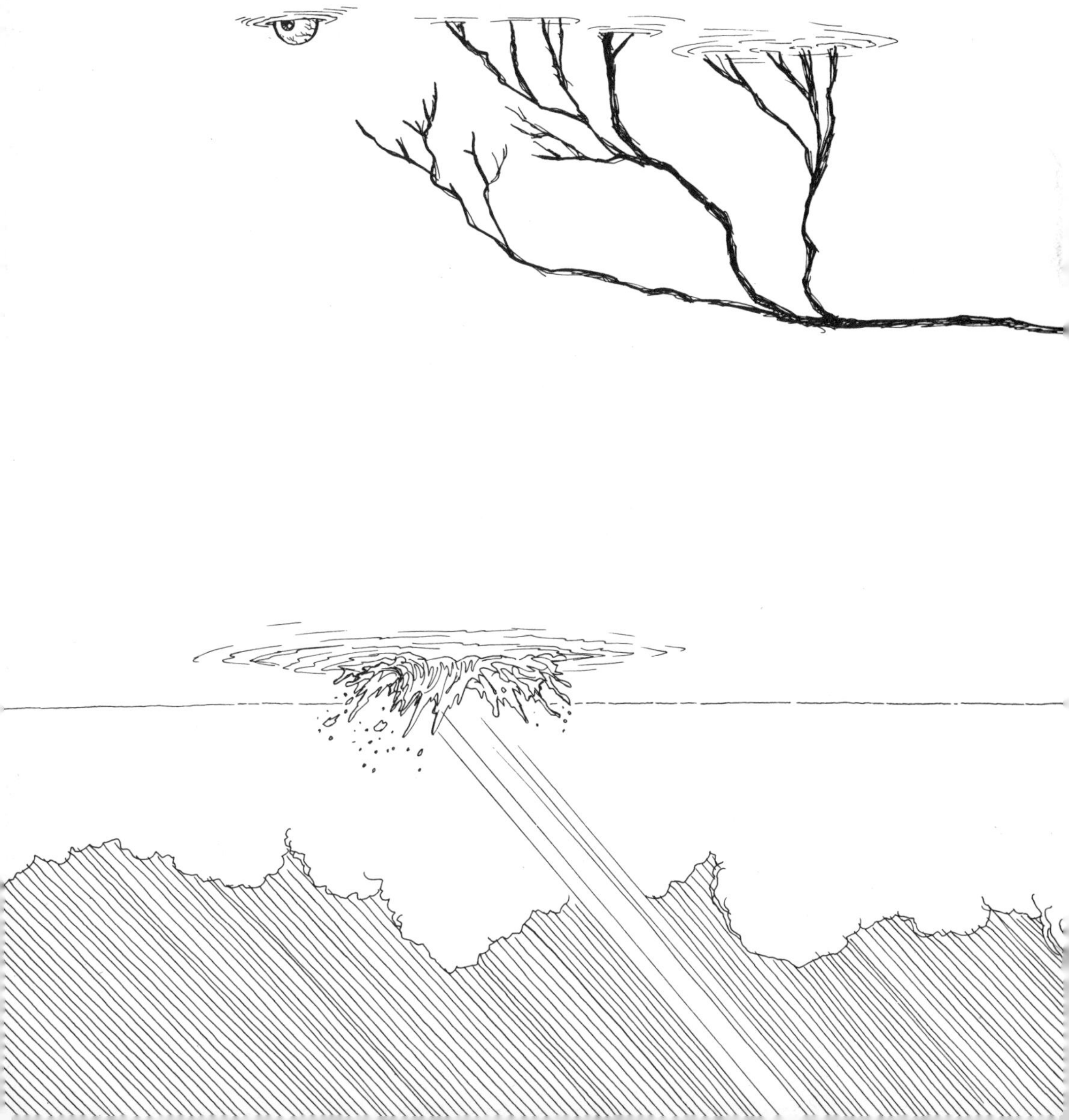

CHARACTERS

IVY

A young Mollie, who along with her Korgi cub Sprout, embark on adventures around Korgi Hollow.

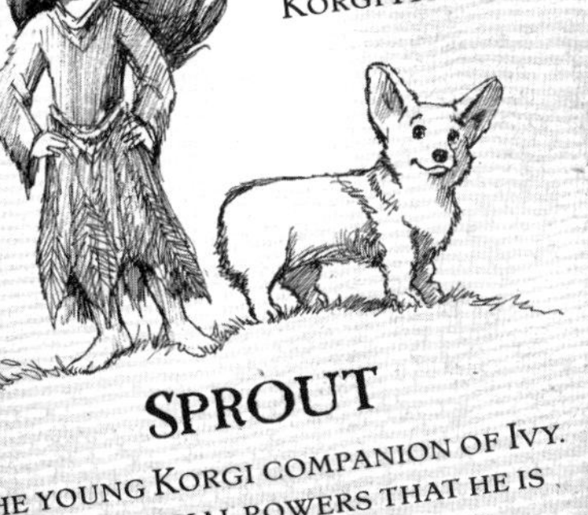

SPROUT

The young Korgi companion of Ivy. He has special powers that he is just now discovering.

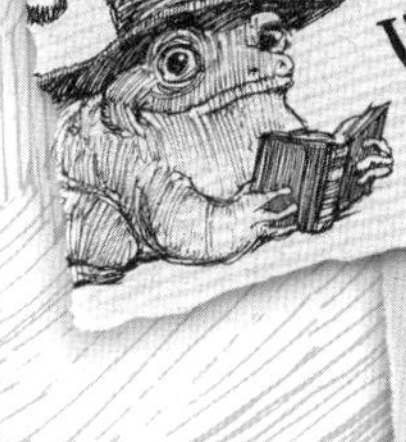

WART

Scrollkeeper and historian of Korgi Hollow.

LUMP

A kind creature who watches over Korgi Hollow.

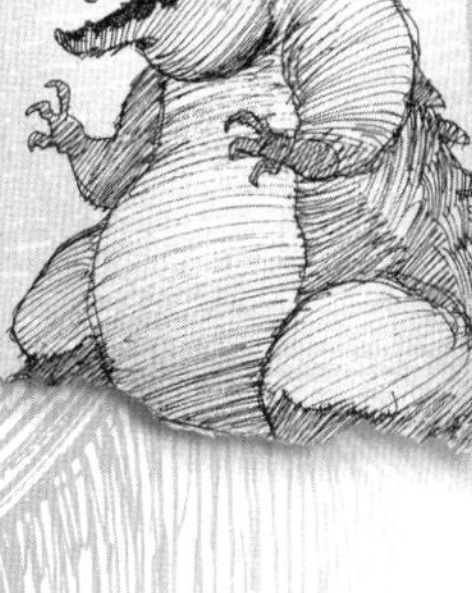

CREEPHOG

Mysterious creatures of an unknown origin who spy on Ivy and Sprout.

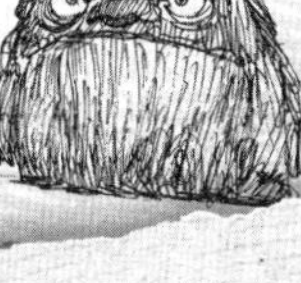

KORGIS

Loyal, fox-like creatures with big ears and large smiles, who live with the mollies in Korgi Hollow.

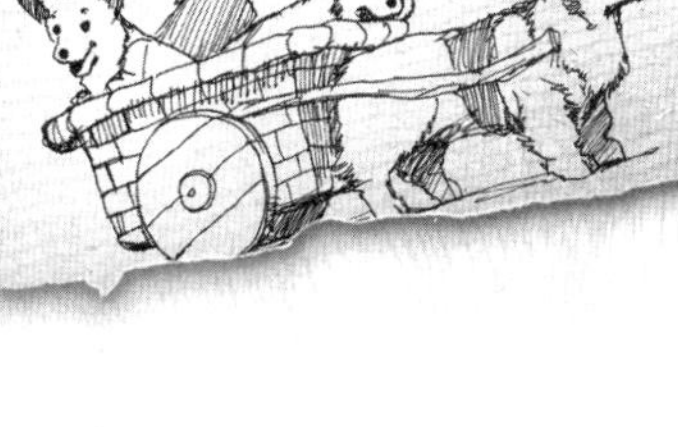

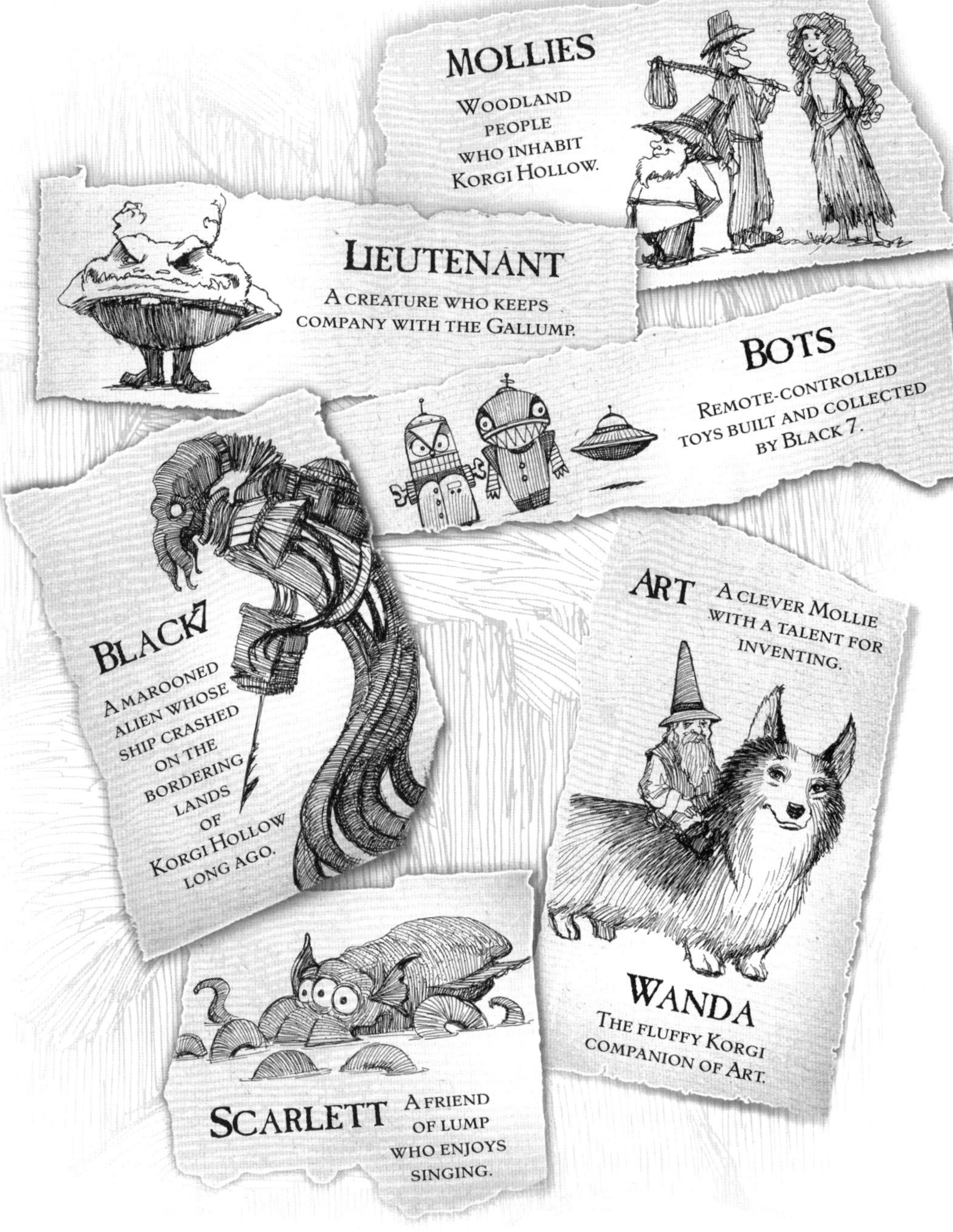
MOLLIES
WOODLAND PEOPLE WHO INHABIT KORGI HOLLOW.
LIEUTENANT
A CREATURE WHO KEEPS COMPANY WITH THE GALLUMP.
BOTS
REMOTE-CONTROLLED TOYS BUILT AND COLLECTED BY BLACK 7.
BLACK7
A MAROONED ALIEN WHOSE SHIP CRASHED ON THE BORDERING LANDS OF KORGI HOLLOW LONG AGO.
ART
A CLEVER MOLLIE WITH A TALENT FOR INVENTING.
WANDA
THE FLUFFY KORGI COMPANION OF ART.
SCARLETT
A FRIEND OF LUMP WHO ENJOYS SINGING.